STAR WARS®

INCREDIBLE CROSS-SECTIONS

WRITTEN BY
DAVID WEST REYNOLDS

ILLUSTRATED BY
HANS JENSSEN
&
RICHARD CHASEMORE

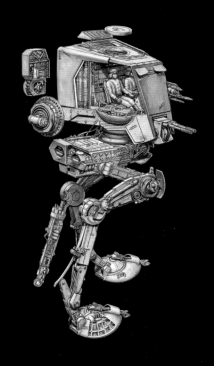

DK PUBLISHING, INC.

CONTENTS

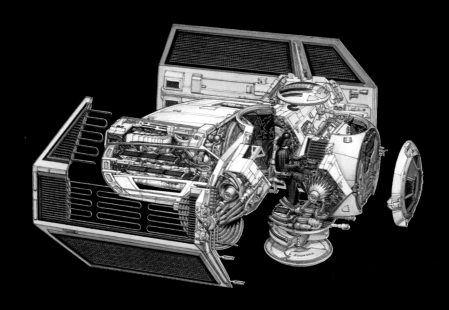

INTRODUCTION

THE DAZZLING SPACECRAFT and exotic vehicles of *Star Wars* soar across our movie screens, almost becoming characters themselves with their intricate detail and fascinating designs. The richness of their conception invites curiosity: what's inside a Jawa sandcrawler, and how does a Star Destroyer deploy its TIE fighters? Where was Ben Kenobi when he deactivated the Death Star's tractor beam? Here at last are revealed the interior layouts and components of these amazing vessels, answering all these questions and more, showing where all the action takes place and how their systems function. The most meticulously detailed research and design work was undertaken to make the extraordinary illustrations of this book definitive. You can spot Chewbacca's bowcaster in the main hold of the *Millennium Falcon*, and you can see in Boba Fett's *Slave I* bunk the data book in which he has finally registered Han Solo as "captured." Many of these craft have been mysteries; their secrets are now unveiled. Explore them for yourself, and revel in the depth of one of the great stories of our age.

SPACECRAFT ENGINES

The advanced engine technology of *Star Wars* takes many forms. Repulsorlifts are safe and reliable devices that lift a ship from the ground and take it into the upper atmosphere of a planet, cushioning its landing upon return. Sublight drives are more intricate and powerful thrust engines, which are used for navigating a ship in the space around a planet. Finally, complex hyperdrive engines use a trans-physical effect to take a ship out of real space into hyperspace, allowing travel between distant stars. It can only be engaged when a ship is clear of a planet's gravity.

SUBLIGHT DRIVES

Spacecraft engage their sublight engines once they are well clear of any facilities or personnel that might be harmed by the mildly radioactive emissions. A variety of sublight engine designs exploit the principle of ion thrust, achieved through various reactants and electronic accelerators from potent fuel mixtures. Fuels can take the form of pressurized radioactive gas, volatile composite fluids, or explosive liquid metal. Acceleration compensators project appropriately modified gravity effects within a spacecraft to preserve pilots and passengers from forceful sublight acceleration.

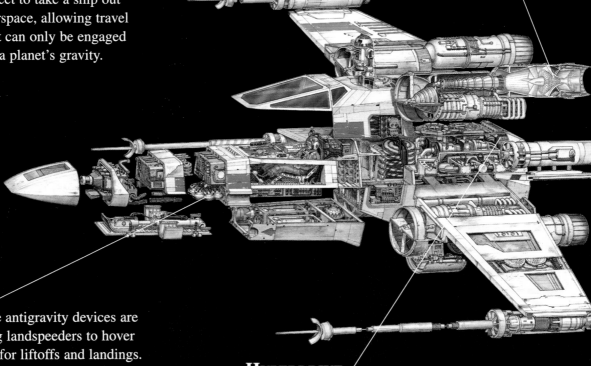

REPULSORLIFTS

These low-maintenance antigravity devices are commonplace, allowing landspeeders to hover and guiding spacecraft for liftoffs and landings. They can even be built into floating droids, although the miniaturized power systems for these are so expensive that they are only used by the Empire. Repulsorlift airspeeders and other such ground-based craft are strictly limited in the altitudes they can reach, with most speeders offering only 2-50 meters of "float." Flight-grade repulsorlifts can carry a vehicle to suborbital altitudes, but only true spacecraft employ these powerful devices.

HYPERDRIVE

Employing an energy effect rather than the matter emissions of sublight engines, hyperdrives are built in many configurations, emphasizing either power, reliability, or lower energy use … no one engine can offer every advantage at once. The multiple components of a hyperdrive system may be located in one area or built into several quarters of a ship for easier maintenance access. Navigation through hyperspace involves extremely complex calculations. Daring pilots may cheat these calculations beyond safety margins, cutting dangerously close to the hyperspace "mass shadows" of real-space bodies, as Han Solo did when he made his notorious impossibly fast Kessel Run.

BLOCKADE RUNNER

PRINCESS LEIA ORGANA OF ALDERAAN travels far and wide on board her consular starship *Tantive IV,* negotiating peace settlements and bringing aid to imperiled populations. Commanded by the daring and loyal Captain Antilles, Leia's *Tantive IV* is a Corellian Corvette: an older, hand-crafted ship of a make seen throughout the galaxy, and famous for its versatility. Under the cover of diplomatic immunity, the senator-princess uses her ship for missions of espionage against the Empire and covert communications for the Rebel Alliance. The *Tantive IV*'s mission profile takes it into both war zones and high-level diplomacy, making its added armor plate as vital as its formal state conference chamber. This sturdy ship has brought the young princess through many harrowing adventures, and it is only under the pursuit of Darth Vader that the *Tantive IV* is finally overtaken and captured.

ESCAPE PODS

Spacecraft escape pods range from coffin-like capsules to large lifeboats which are small ships in their own right. The Blockade Runner carries eight small escape pods rated for up to three people, and four laser-armed pods which seat 12. More sophisticated than the smaller pods, these lifeboats nonetheless have a very limited range. None of the *Tantive IV*'s escape systems could save its crew from the *Devastator*'s guns.

Armed high-capacity escape pod doubles as long-range laser turret

Added armor plate permanently covers stateroom windows

Formal dining room

High-capacity pod is boarded via central access ladder

Mid-ship elevator

Leia's stateroom suite

Control and power linkages

Officers' briefing room

Officers' quarters

Forward elevator

Computer power substation

Formal state conference chamber

Tech station monitors ship operations

Leia's seat

Darth Vader throttles Captain Antilles

Cockpit

Operations forum

Rebel prisoners and droids being escorted off the ship for interrogation

Escape pod access tunnel

Commander Praji in main computer room

Captain Antilles' quarters

Escape pod that C-3PO and R2-D2 will use

Forward airlock docking hatch

Lower turbolaser is manned by two gunners

Defensive field projector

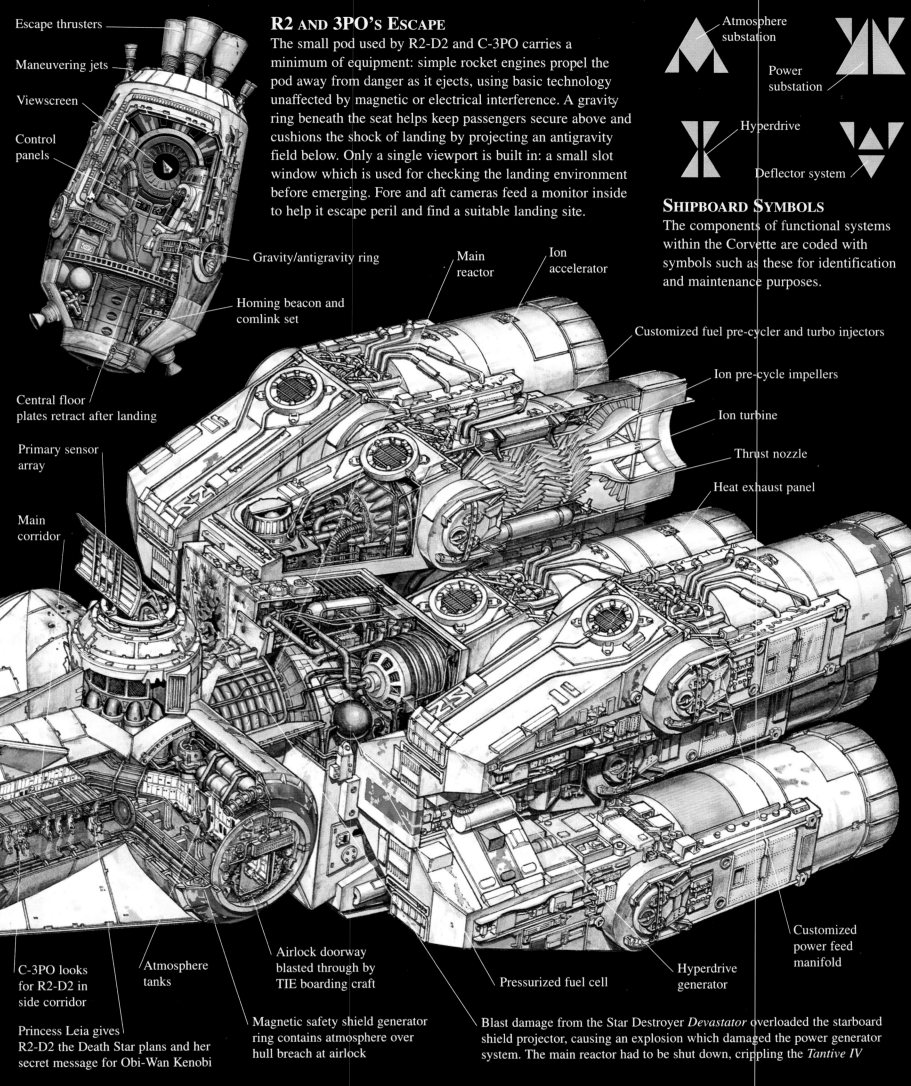

Escape thrusters

Maneuvering jets

Viewscreen

Control panels

R2 AND 3PO'S ESCAPE
The small pod used by R2-D2 and C-3PO carries a minimum of equipment: simple rocket engines propel the pod away from danger as it ejects, using basic technology unaffected by magnetic or electrical interference. A gravity ring beneath the seat helps keep passengers secure above and cushions the shock of landing by projecting an antigravity field below. Only a single viewport is built in: a small slot window which is used for checking the landing environment before emerging. Fore and aft cameras feed a monitor inside to help it escape peril and find a suitable landing site.

Atmosphere substation

Power substation

Hyperdrive

Deflector system

SHIPBOARD SYMBOLS
The components of functional systems within the Corvette are coded with symbols such as these for identification and maintenance purposes.

Gravity/antigravity ring

Homing beacon and comlink set

Central floor plates retract after landing

Primary sensor array

Main corridor

Main reactor

Ion accelerator

Customized fuel pre-cycler and turbo injectors

Ion pre-cycle impellers

Ion turbine

Thrust nozzle

Heat exhaust panel

C-3PO looks for R2-D2 in side corridor

Princess Leia gives R2-D2 the Death Star plans and her secret message for Obi-Wan Kenobi

Atmosphere tanks

Airlock doorway blasted through by TIE boarding craft

Magnetic safety shield generator ring contains atmosphere over hull breach at airlock

Pressurized fuel cell

Hyperdrive generator

Customized power feed manifold

Blast damage from the Star Destroyer *Devastator* overloaded the starboard shield projector, causing an explosion which damaged the power generator system. The main reactor had to be shut down, crippling the *Tantive IV*

THE CAPABLE CORVETTE
Sporting twin turbolaser turrets and a massive drive block of eleven ion turbine engines for speed, the Corellian Corvette balances defensive capabilities with a high power-to-mass ratio, meaning that what it can't shoot down it can generally outrun. These capable ships have been adapted to many uses, from cargo and passenger transport to scientific and military applications, but their most notorious use is in the hands of Corellian smugglers.

CONTRABANDITS
Blending anonymously into galactic space traffic, Corellian smugglers skillfully pilot their multi-engined Corvettes through Imperial security zones to avoid duties and taxes (or arrest for dealing in weapons and illegal goods). They are hard to spot, and chagrined Imperial officials have given the make its nickname "Blockade Runner."

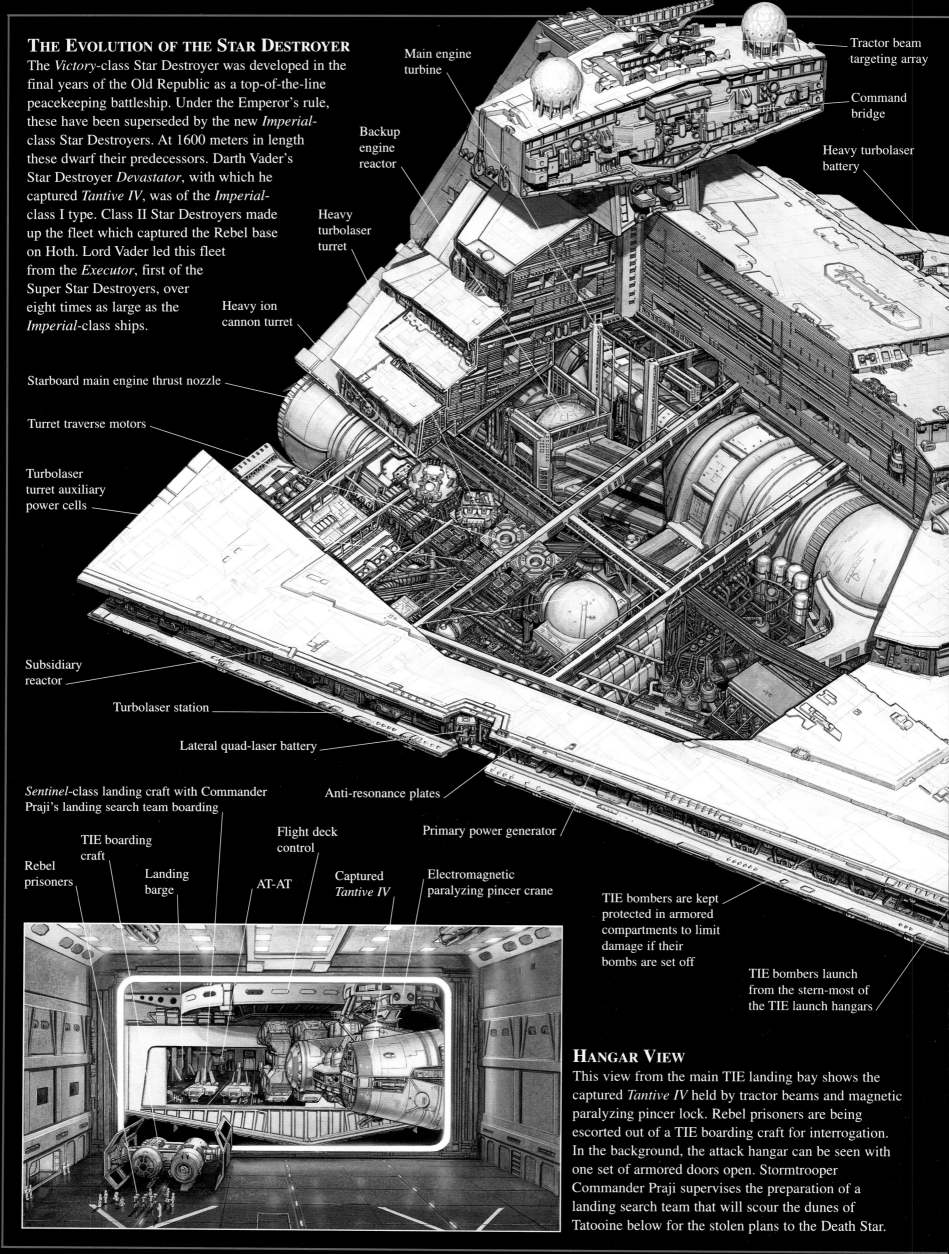

THE EVOLUTION OF THE STAR DESTROYER

The *Victory*-class Star Destroyer was developed in the final years of the Old Republic as a top-of-the-line peacekeeping battleship. Under the Emperor's rule, these have been superseded by the new *Imperial*-class Star Destroyers. At 1600 meters in length these dwarf their predecessors. Darth Vader's Star Destroyer *Devastator*, with which he captured *Tantive IV*, was of the *Imperial*-class I type. Class II Star Destroyers made up the fleet which captured the Rebel base on Hoth. Lord Vader led this fleet from the *Executor*, first of the Super Star Destroyers, over eight times as large as the *Imperial*-class ships.

Main engine turbine

Tractor beam targeting array

Command bridge

Heavy turbolaser battery

Backup engine reactor

Heavy turbolaser turret

Heavy ion cannon turret

Starboard main engine thrust nozzle

Turret traverse motors

Turbolaser turret auxiliary power cells

Subsidiary reactor

Turbolaser station

Lateral quad-laser battery

Sentinel-class landing craft with Commander Praji's landing search team boarding

TIE boarding craft

Rebel prisoners

Landing barge

AT-AT

Flight deck control

Captured *Tantive IV*

Anti-resonance plates

Primary power generator

Electromagnetic paralyzing pincer crane

TIE bombers are kept protected in armored compartments to limit damage if their bombs are set off

TIE bombers launch from the stern-most of the TIE launch hangars

HANGAR VIEW

This view from the main TIE landing bay shows the captured *Tantive IV* held by tractor beams and magnetic paralyzing pincer lock. Rebel prisoners are being escorted out of a TIE boarding craft for interrogation. In the background, the attack hangar can be seen with one set of armored doors open. Stormtrooper Commander Praji supervises the preparation of a landing search team that will scour the dunes of Tatooine below for the stolen plans to the Death Star.

STAR DESTROYER

THE STAR DESTROYER is a symbol of the Empire's military might, carrying devastating firepower and assault forces anywhere in the galaxy to subjugate opposition. A Star Destroyer can easily overtake most fleeing craft, blasting them into submission or drawing them into its main hangar with tractor beams. *Imperial*-class Star Destroyers are 1600 meters long, bristling with turbolasers and ion cannons, and equipped with eight giant turret gun stations. Star Destroyers carry 9700 stormtroopers and a full wing of 72 TIE ships (typically including 48 TIE/In fighters, 12 TIE bombers, and 12 TIE boarding craft) as well as a range of attack and landing craft. A single Star Destroyer can overwhelm an entire rebellious planet. Major industrialized worlds are assaulted with a fleet of six Star Destroyers operating with support cruisers and supply craft. Such a force can obliterate any defenses, occupying or completely destroying cities or settlements.

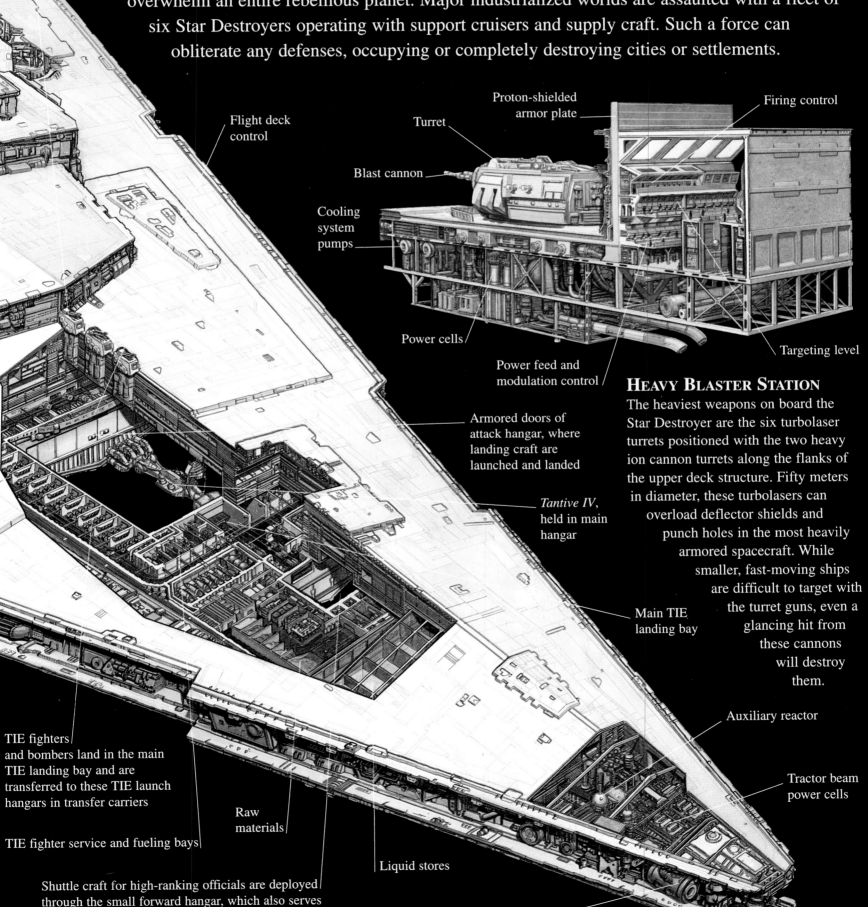

Axial defense turret

Flight deck control

Proton-shielded armor plate

Firing control

Turret

Blast cannon

Cooling system pumps

Power cells

Power feed and modulation control

Armored doors of attack hangar, where landing craft are launched and landed

Tantive IV, held in main hangar

Main TIE landing bay

Targeting level

HEAVY BLASTER STATION
The heaviest weapons on board the Star Destroyer are the six turbolaser turrets positioned with the two heavy ion cannon turrets along the flanks of the upper deck structure. Fifty meters in diameter, these turbolasers can overload deflector shields and punch holes in the most heavily armored spacecraft. While smaller, fast-moving ships are difficult to target with the turret guns, even a glancing hit from these cannons will destroy them.

Auxiliary reactor

Tractor beam power cells

TIE fighters and bombers land in the main TIE landing bay and are transferred to these TIE launch hangars in transfer carriers

TIE fighter service and fueling bays

Raw materials

Liquid stores

Shuttle craft for high-ranking officials are deployed through the small forward hangar, which also serves as back-up to the main hangar

Pursuit tractor beams

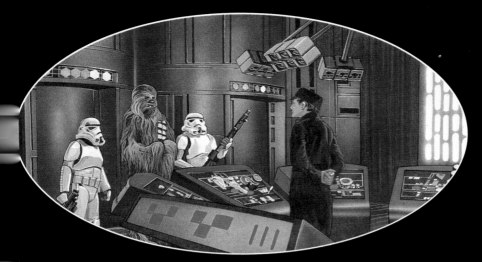

DETENTION BLOCK AA-23

A desperate plan takes Luke, Han, and Chewbacca into the heart of peril as they try to rescue Princess Leia. Disguised as stormtroopers, Luke and Han escort Chewbacca, their "prisoner," into Leia's detention block. The supervisor suspects trouble, and only immediate action will save the Rebels.

TRASH COMPACTOR 32-6-3827

Escaping Leia's cell block, the Rebels dive into a garbage chute and land in a trash compactor, where refuse of every kind is collected before being processed and dumped into space.

AIR SHAFT

Throughout the Death Star are vast air shafts. Extensible bridges connect passages across the shafts, but can be disabled. When Luke and Leia find themselves trapped at one of the air shafts, quick thinking and bravery provide the only way across.

TRACTOR BEAM REACTOR COUPLING

The Death Star tractor beam is coupled to the main reactor in seven locations. These power terminals stand atop generator towers 35 kilometers tall. The air is taut with high-voltage electricity throughout the shaft surrounding the tower. It is in this setting that Ben Kenobi secretly deactivates one of the power beams to allow the *Millennium Falcon* to escape.

CHALLENGE AND SACRIFICE

Darth Vader senses the presence of his old Jedi master Obi-Wan Kenobi aboard the Death Star, and confronts him alone in a deadly lightsaber duel. Kenobi sacrifices himself to help his young friends escape, yielding to Vader in an empty victory in which, mysteriously, Obi-Wan becomes one with the Force.

Power processing networks

Navigational beacon

Atmosphere processing unit

Control room window

Hallway overlook windows

Ion drive reactor

Turbolaser turret

Atmosphere processing substation

Ben Kenobi and Darth Vader

Equatorial docking bay

Landing alignment marking

Ion sublight engines

DOCKING BAY 3207

Drawn in by a tractor beam, the *Millennium Falcon* comes to rest in a pressurized hangar within the Death Star's equatorial trench. Magnetic shields over the entrance retain the atmosphere. Outboard power-feeds hook up to landed craft so that the ship reactors can be shut down while in the hangar.

DEATH STAR

THE EMPIRE'S GIGANTIC battle station code named Death Star is 160 kilometers in diameter, large enough to be mistaken for a small moon. The brainchild of Grand Moff Tarkin, this colossal super-weapon is designed to enforce the Emperor's rule through terror, presenting both the symbol and reality of ultimate destructive power. Making use of the Empire's most advanced discoveries in super-engineering, the Death Star is built around a hypermatter reactor which can generate enough power to destroy an entire planet. Constructed in secret by slave labor and titanic factory machines, the Death Star's vast structure houses millions of soldiers and thousands of armed spacecraft, making it capable of occupying whole star systems by force. Elite gunners and troopers man the station's advanced weapons. The Death Star, once fully operational, represents a chilling specter of totalitarian domination and threatens to extinguish all hope for freedom in the galaxy.

CRUCIAL WEAKNESS

The Death Star's powerful defenses have one fatal flaw – small thermal exhaust ports that lead from the surface to the heart of the main reactor.

Main exhaust port

Thermal exhaust port shaft runs through central power column

Equatorial trench

Inner decks stacked

Surface decks concentric

THE STOLEN PLANS

A complete technical readout of the battle station (left) was stolen by Rebel spies. These plans reveal the overwhelming might of the Death Star, detailing its myriad weapons systems and immense power structures. Ion engines, hyperdrives, and hangar bays ring the station's equatorial trench, while power cells over 15 kilometers wide distribute energy throughout the thousands of internal decks of the station. Air shafts and void spaces honeycomb the interior. Occupying the polar axis of the Death Star is its central power column, with the hypermatter reactor at its core.

ALDERAAN DESTROYED

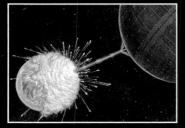

Without hesitation Grand Moff Tarkin orders the destruction of the peaceful planet Alderaan as the first demonstration of the Death Star's power. As the superlaser lances out at the blue-green planet, this horrific act wipes out billions of people.

SUPERLASER TRIBUTARY BEAM SHAFT

Eight tributary beams unite to form the superlaser primary beam. These tributary beams are arranged around the invisible central focusing field, firing in alternate sequence to build the power necessary to destroy a planet. The titanic energy of these beams must be monitored to prevent imbalance explosions.

TIE FIGHTER

HURTLING THROUGH SPACE, TIE fighters are the most visible image of the Empire's wide-reaching power. The TIE fighter engine is the most precisely manufactured propulsion system in the galaxy. Solar ionization collects light energy and channels it through a reactor to fire emissions from a high-pressure radioactive gas. The engine has no moving parts, making it low-maintenance. To reduce the mass of the ship, TIE fighters are built without defensive shields, hyperdrive capability, and life support systems – so the pilots must wear spacesuits. The light-weight ship gains speed and maneuverability at the price of fragility and dependence on nearby Imperial bases or larger craft for support.

ALL THE SAME

TIE pilots may never use the same ship twice, and develop no sentimental attachment to their craft as Rebels often do. TIE pilots know that every reconditioned fighter is identical to a factory-fresh ship; one is the same as many thousands – another reinforcement of Imperial philosophy of absolute conformity.

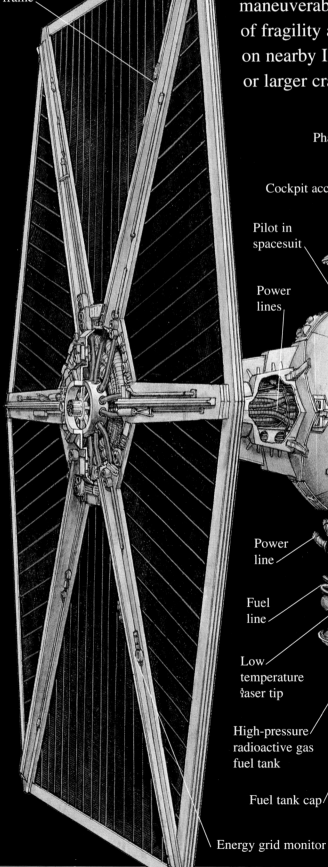

Solar energy collectors

Solar array support frame

Energy accumulator lines

Heat exchange matrix

Phase two energy collection coils

Cockpit access hatch

Main viewport

Pilot in spacesuit

Power lines

Power line

Fuel line

Low temperature laser tip

High-pressure radioactive gas fuel tank

Fuel tank cap

Energy grid monitor

TIE MISSION PROFILES

TIE fighters are deployed for a variety of mission profiles. Their primary role is as space superiority fighters, engaging Rebel craft and defending Imperial bases and capital ships. Scout TIEs may travel alone to cover wide areas of space. Such individual scouts patrol the huge asteroid field left by the explosion of the planet Alderaan. Ships are assigned to escort duty in pairs, such as the twin TIEs that escort all flights of the Emperor's shuttle. Regular sentry groups of four TIE fighters patrol the space around Imperial bases, stations, and capital starships. A typical TIE fighter attack squadron consists of 12 ships, and a full attack wing consists of six squadrons, or 72 TIE fighters.

TIE VARIANTS

The basic structure of the TIE fighter has proven so successful that derivative variants use the same cockpit, wing brace structure, and drive system components. The Advanced X1 (above center) added shields and hyperdrive. The fearsome TIE Interceptor (above right) features improved ion drives and electronics, and advanced ion stream projectors giving exceptional control.

Retaining claw

Launching TIE fighter

TIE in ready launch position

Pilots' boarding gantry

Transfer tunnel

Pilot boarding ship

TIE arriving from landing hangar

Service droid

Hangar control room

Elevator well

Service gantry

TIE HANGAR

TIEs are launched from cycling racks of up to 72 ships in the larger hangars; smaller hangars may contain as few as two ships. Pilots board from overhead gantries and are released to space as they disengage from the front position in the rack system. Returning ships land in separate hangars, where they are guided into receiver-carriers by small tractor beams. The receivers carry the TIE to a debarkation station where the pilot exits. From there the TIE may be serviced and refueled in a separate bay on its way through transfer tunnels to a launch hangar. In the launch hangar the TIE is cycled into the launch rack, ready for its next mission.

PILOT PSYCHOLOGY

TIE fighters lack landing gear, a measure designed to reduce mass for maximum maneuverability. While the ships are structurally capable of sitting on their wings, they are not designed to land or disembark pilots without special support. This teaches the pilots to rely completely on higher authority.

Tractor beam generator tower

Beam emitter crystal

Overbridge

Star Destroyer

Primary beam focusing magnet

Main power generator

Targeting field generator

Static discharge tower

Carrier beam crystal

Hail of fire

Darth Vader's TIE fighter

Surface turbolaser tower

Magnetic shielding

Hyperdrive

Tributary superlaser beam shaft

Induction hyperphase generator

Firing field amplifier

Primary power amplifier

Insulator plating

Hypermatter reactor

ASSAULT ON THE POLAR TRENCH

The exhaust port target of the Rebel assault is protected in a trench, which is in turn protected by a hail of fire from deadly turbolaser towers on the Death Star surface. To bomb the exhaust port, the Rebel fighters must maneuver down the trench beneath the fire zone, but they find themselves pursued closely by Imperial TIE fighters and Darth Vader himself. The defense is lethal: all but three of the Rebel fighters are destroyed.

Docking Bay 3207

OVERBRIDGE

The primary control room of the Death Star is the overbridge, situated at the top edge of the superlaser dish. From this nerve center Grand Moff Tarkin commands the gigantic battle station. The staff feeds critical information to the main viewscreen.

EXHAUST PORT

The Rebels target this two-meter-wide thermal exhaust port as their one chance of destroying the Death Star. Red Leader's shot at the small port is only a near miss.

Tractor beam power coupling
deactivated by Ben Kenobi

Target exhaust
shaft

Concentric surface structure

Power cell

Secondary power
converters

SANDCRAWLER

A LEFTOVER TITAN from a forgotten mining era long ago, the Jawa sandcrawler patrols the deserts and wastelands of Tatooine in search of metal salvage and minerals. Serving as home to an entire clan of Jawas, the mobile sandcrawler makes its rounds across wide territory over the course of a year, hunting for the wrecks that dot Tatooine's surface from spaceship crashes through centuries past. Jawas also round up stray droids, junked vehicles, and unwanted metal of any kind from settlements and moisture farmers. Pitted and scoured by numberless sandstorms, the sandcrawler serves the Jawas as transportation, workshop, traveling store, and safe protection from the menaces of Sand People and desert monsters.

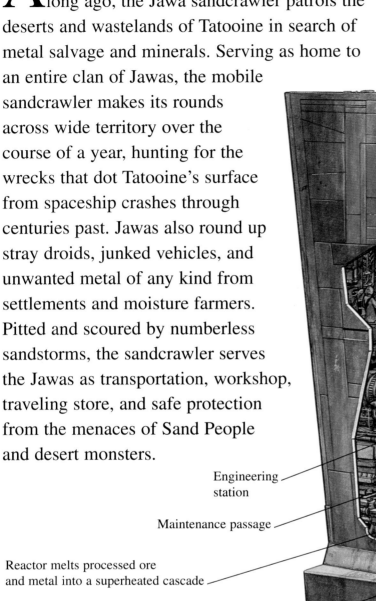

Case-hardened smashers crush minerals or compact metal for storage

Conveyor at top of elevator

Drill grinders

Laser pre-processor

Power generators

Ore crusher

Reactor powers entire sandcrawler

Engineering station

Maintenance passage

Reactor melts processed ore and metal into a superheated cascade

Power cells

Ingots are extruded from purified underlevels of slag pool

Primary drive

Rear treads non-steerable, for drive only

Electrostatic repellers keep sand from interior components

Steam-heating array

Repulsorlift tube energizer

Extensible starboard boarding gantry

Extensible repulsorlift tube

JAWA REPAIRS

Jawas are experts at making use of available components to repair machinery and can put together a working droid from the most surprising variety of scrap parts. However, they are notorious for peddling shoddy workmanship that will last just long enough for the sandcrawler to disappear over the horizon.

DANGEROUS PRIZES

The furious winds of Tatooine's storm season can scour ancient spacewrecks from the deep sands of the Dune Sea. Jawa sandcrawlers venture into extremely remote territories after the big storms in search of newly exposed prizes. Larger finds may cause them to call in other clan sandcrawlers to share in the processing. Field smelting factories and sun shelter awnings are quickly erected as the Jawas work to beat the arrival of the next storm. But the wastelands can hold dangers more unexpected than storms.

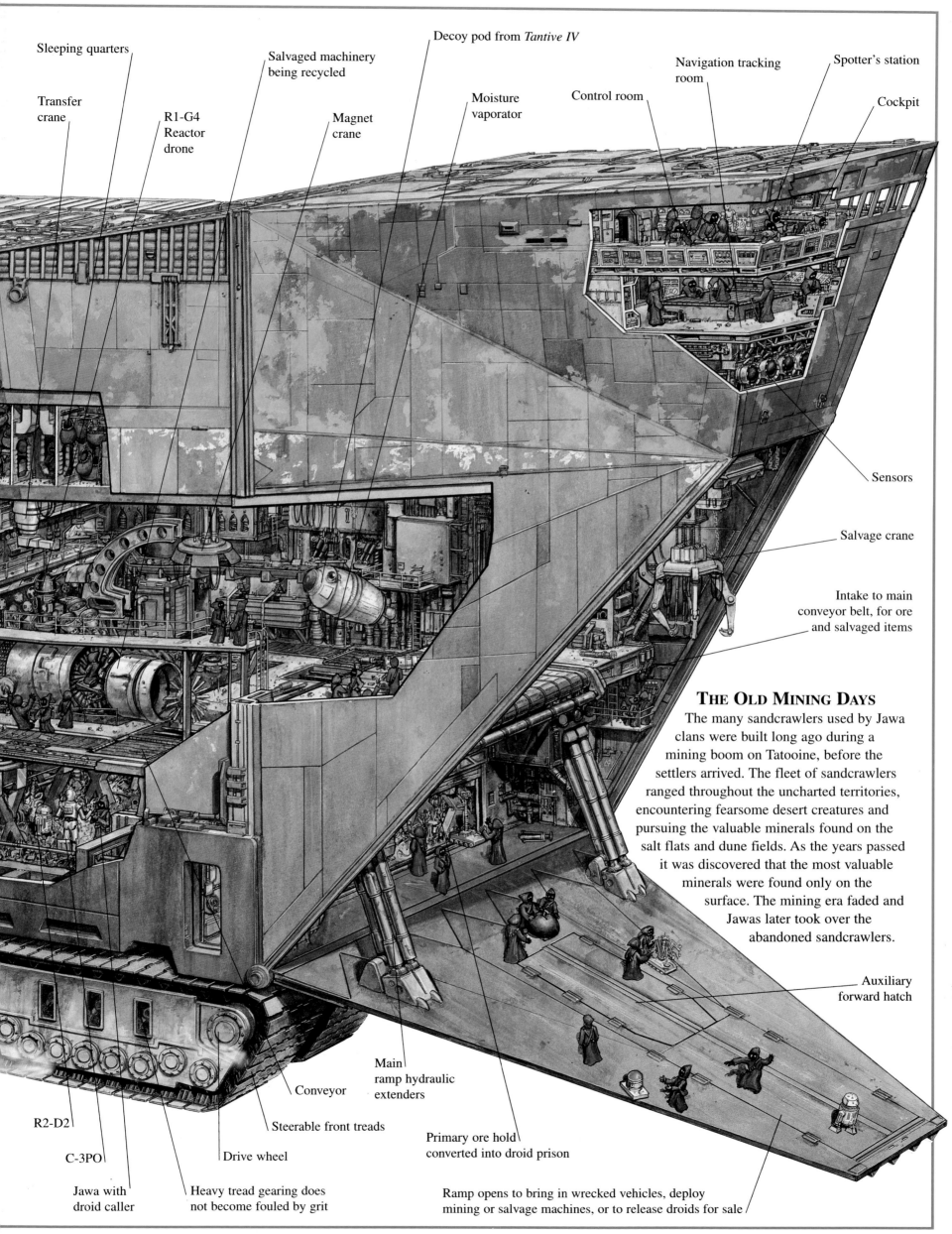

Sleeping quarters

Transfer crane

R1-G4 Reactor drone

Salvaged machinery being recycled

Magnet crane

Decoy pod from *Tantive IV*

Moisture vaporator

Control room

Navigation tracking room

Spotter's station

Cockpit

Sensors

Salvage crane

Intake to main conveyor belt, for ore and salvaged items

THE OLD MINING DAYS

The many sandcrawlers used by Jawa clans were built long ago during a mining boom on Tatooine, before the settlers arrived. The fleet of sandcrawlers ranged throughout the uncharted territories, encountering fearsome desert creatures and pursuing the valuable minerals found on the salt flats and dune fields. As the years passed it was discovered that the most valuable minerals were found only on the surface. The mining era faded and Jawas later took over the abandoned sandcrawlers.

Auxiliary forward hatch

R2-D2

C-3PO

Jawa with droid caller

Heavy tread gearing does not become fouled by grit

Drive wheel

Steerable front treads

Conveyor

Main ramp hydraulic extenders

Primary ore hold converted into droid prison

Ramp opens to bring in wrecked vehicles, deploy mining or salvage machines, or to release droids for sale

MILLENNIUM FALCON

BATTERED, SCARRED, AND MUCH-MODIFIED, Han Solo's *Millennium Falcon* looks more like a bad scrap job than one of the fastest spaceships in the galaxy. This remarkable Corellian pirate ship began its life as a YT-1300 stock light freighter, but like many ships of its class the *Falcon* went through significant remodeling at the hands of smuggler captains. Its engines have doubled in size, its defenses are military-grade heavy-duty destructive weapons, and in every respect it is a high-performance hot rod of the highest caliber. The extensive modifications bring a price, however, in the form of endless maintenance. Solo makes his living by smuggling everything from weapons to contraband spices through Imperial blockades in the quest for profit outside the Empire's restrictive laws.

A LONG HISTORY

Han Solo won the *Millennium Falcon* from his old friend and fellow smuggler Lando Calrissian in a heated game of sabacc. Lando had no right to complain, having come to own the *Falcon* through gambling in the first place. Over many years, dozens of minor laser hits and micrometeoroid punctures have been patched with micro-panels (or even left alone), giving the ship a dilapidated appearance. Han Solo now refuses to clean up his ship's appearance as a matter of pride.

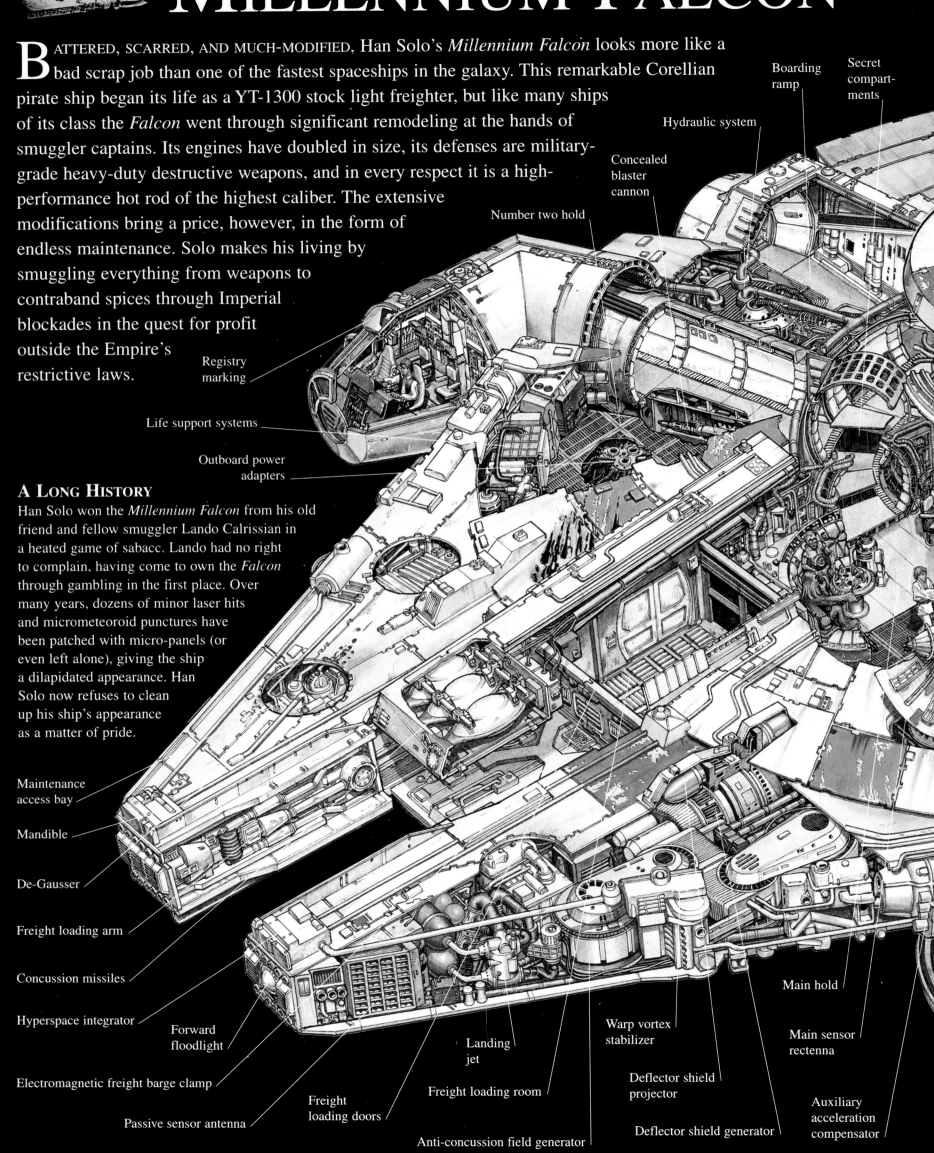

Boarding ramp

Secret compartments

Hydraulic system

Concealed blaster cannon

Number two hold

Registry marking

Life support systems

Outboard power adapters

Maintenance access bay

Mandible

De-Gausser

Freight loading arm

Concussion missiles

Hyperspace integrator

Forward floodlight

Electromagnetic freight barge clamp

Passive sensor antenna

Freight loading doors

Landing jet

Freight loading room

Anti-concussion field generator

Warp vortex stabilizer

Deflector shield projector

Deflector shield generator

Main hold

Main sensor rectenna

Auxiliary acceleration compensator

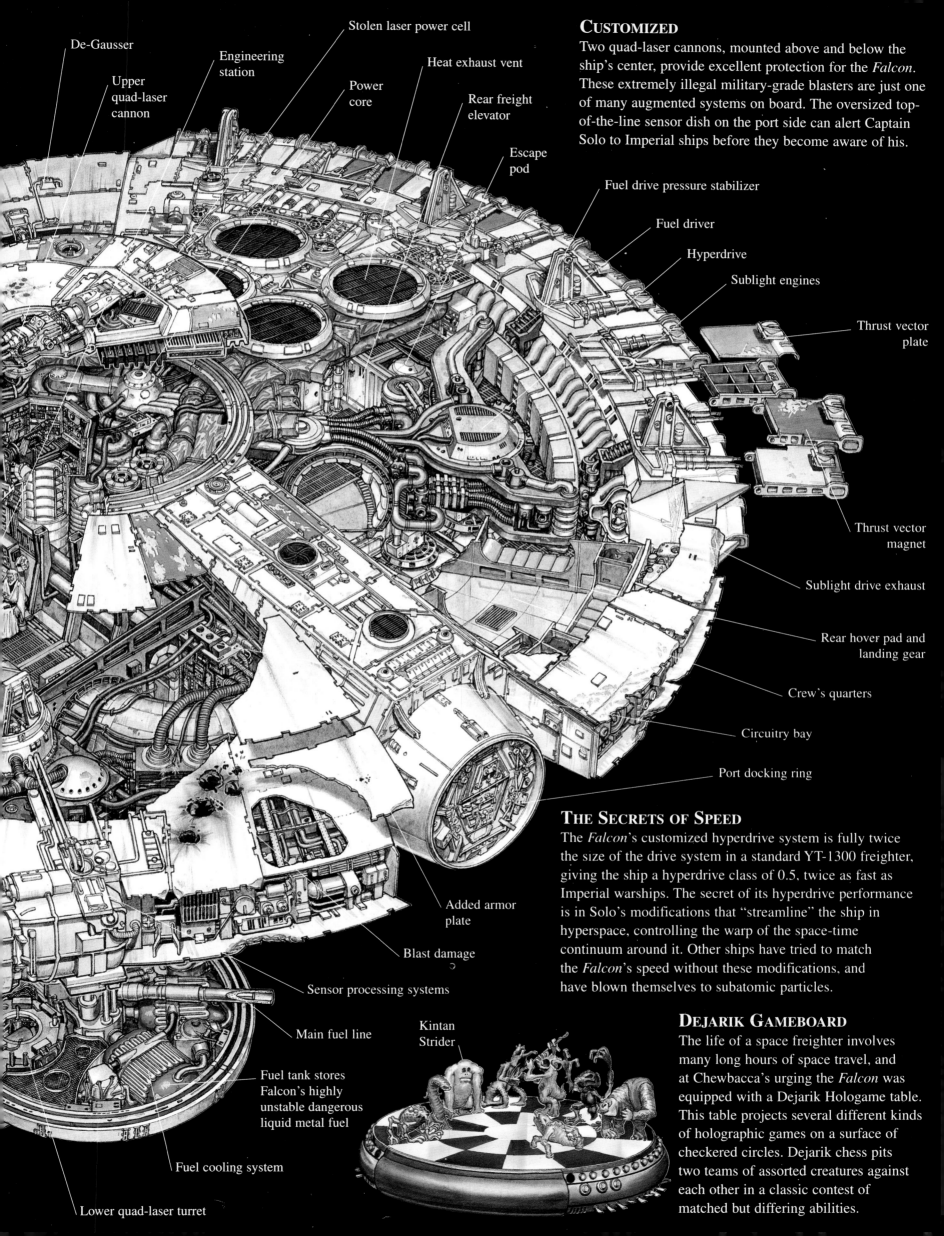

De-Gausser

Upper quad-laser cannon

Engineering station

Stolen laser power cell

Power core

Heat exhaust vent

Rear freight elevator

Escape pod

CUSTOMIZED

Two quad-laser cannons, mounted above and below the ship's center, provide excellent protection for the *Falcon*. These extremely illegal military-grade blasters are just one of many augmented systems on board. The oversized top-of-the-line sensor dish on the port side can alert Captain Solo to Imperial ships before they become aware of his.

Fuel drive pressure stabilizer

Fuel driver

Hyperdrive

Sublight engines

Thrust vector plate

Thrust vector magnet

Sublight drive exhaust

Rear hover pad and landing gear

Crew's quarters

Circuitry bay

Port docking ring

THE SECRETS OF SPEED

The *Falcon*'s customized hyperdrive system is fully twice the size of the drive system in a standard YT-1300 freighter, giving the ship a hyperdrive class of 0.5, twice as fast as Imperial warships. The secret of its hyperdrive performance is in Solo's modifications that "streamline" the ship in hyperspace, controlling the warp of the space-time continuum around it. Other ships have tried to match the *Falcon*'s speed without these modifications, and have blown themselves to subatomic particles.

Added armor plate

Blast damage

Sensor processing systems

Main fuel line

Kintan Strider

Fuel tank stores *Falcon*'s highly unstable dangerous liquid metal fuel

Fuel cooling system

Lower quad-laser turret

DEJARIK GAMEBOARD

The life of a space freighter involves many long hours of space travel, and at Chewbacca's urging the *Falcon* was equipped with a Dejarik Hologame table. This table projects several different kinds of holographic games on a surface of checkered circles. Dejarik chess pits two teams of assorted creatures against each other in a classic contest of matched but differing abilities.

T-65 X-WING

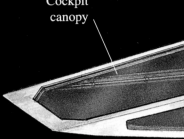

THE X-WING STARFIGHTER was a top-secret project of the Incom Corporation when the Empire began to suspect Rebel sympathies within the company and seized its assets. Key members of the design team escaped with the plans and two prototypes, destroying all other records of the ship. Hence, into the hands of the Rebellion came what would become its finest space fighter. Carrying heavy firepower, hyperdrive, and defensive shields, the X-wing is nonetheless maneuverable enough for close combat with the Empire's lethally agile TIE fighters. A truly formidable space superiority fighter, the X-wing's complex systems and rare alloys have delayed production of significant numbers of the craft for years.

Targeting scope

Primary control systems similar to those of civilian aircraft like the T-16 Skyhopper

INSIDE THE COCKPIT
The X-wing's highly responsive maneuverability can make it a dangerous craft for new pilots to handle. In addition to the fairly straightforward flight control systems, comprehensive cockpit displays allow the pilot to monitor and control energy distribution throughout the ship's systems during combat.

Cockpit canopy

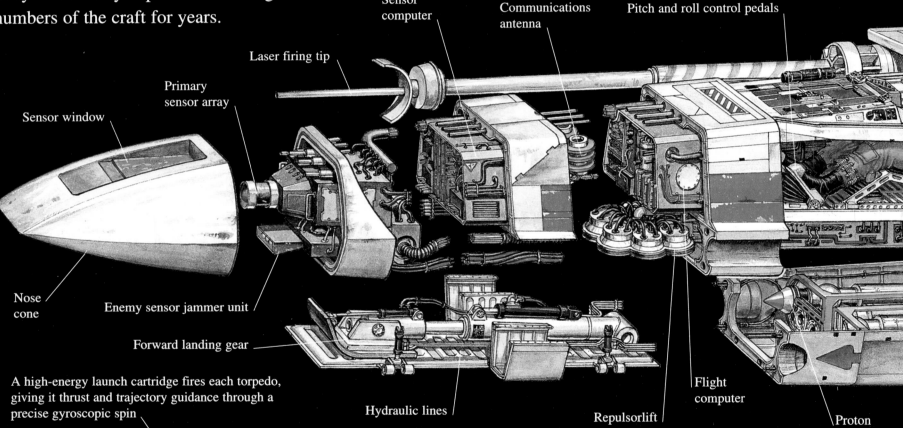

Sensor computer

Communications antenna

Pitch and roll control pedals

Laser firing tip

Primary sensor array

Sensor window

Nose cone

Enemy sensor jammer unit

Forward landing gear

A high-energy launch cartridge fires each torpedo, giving it thrust and trajectory guidance through a precise gyroscopic spin

Hydraulic lines

Flight computer

Repulsorlift

Proton torpedo

Proton warhead

Guidance gyro

Arming power shell

DESTROYER OF THE DEATH STAR
Proton torpedoes such as the MG7-As carried by the X-wing are extremely dangerous focused nuclear explosives. They are used for critical target destruction or to punch through ray shielding that will deflect laser weapons. Proton torpedoes are very expensive and available to Alliance forces only in limited numbers. Luke Skywalker carried only a single pair for his critical shots that destroyed the original Death Star.

INDEPENDENT OPERATION
Hyperdrive and the ability to launch and land without special support enable the X-wing to operate independently, unlike Imperial TIE fighters. The X-wing is equipped with life support sufficient for one week in space: air, water, food, and life-process support equipment are packed into the area behind the pilot's seat. When the ship lands, the air supply can be renewed, and the water and life support systems can be partially recharged. A cargo bay carries survival gear for pilots who land in hostile environments or remote places.

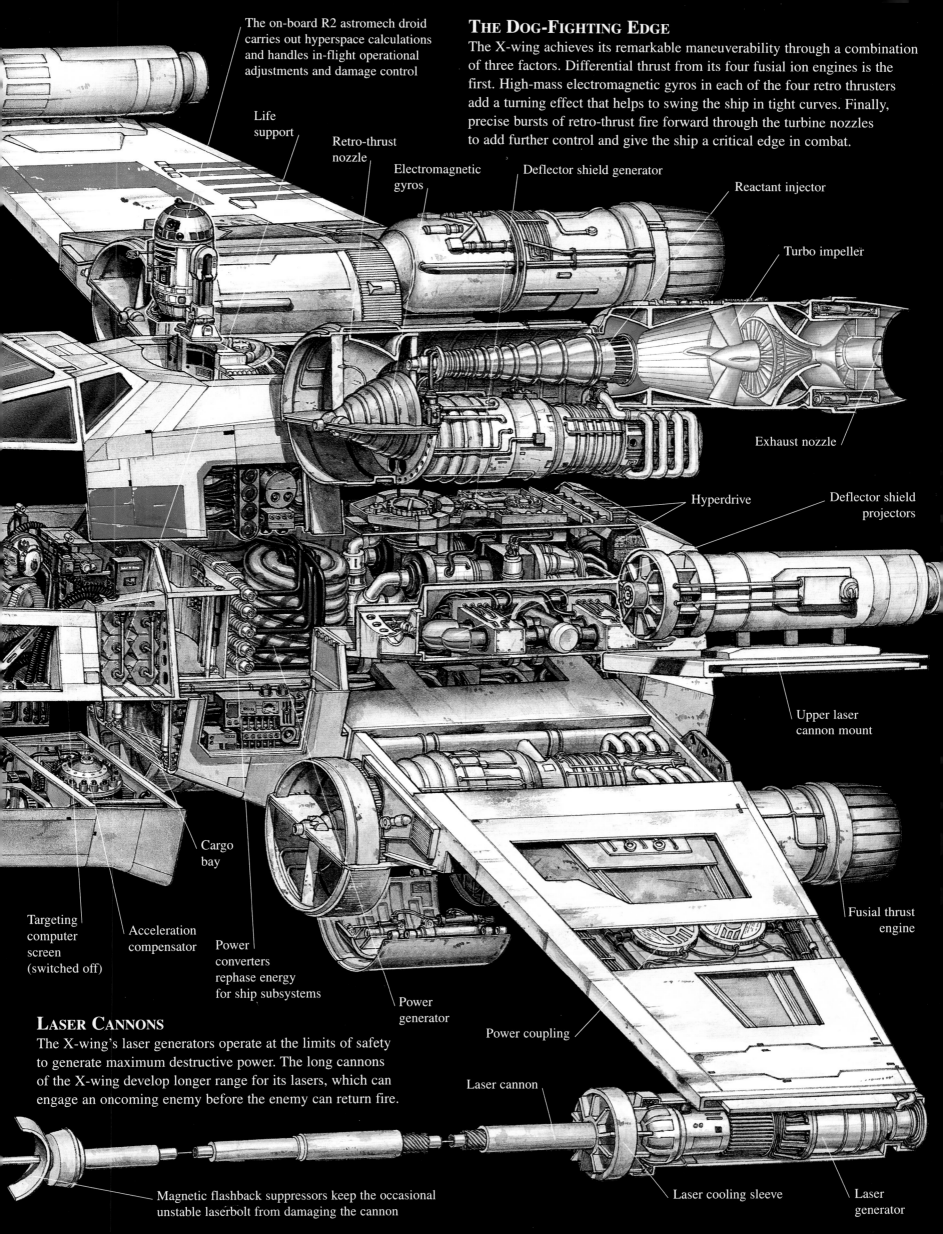

The on-board R2 astromech droid carries out hyperspace calculations and handles in-flight operational adjustments and damage control

Life support

Retro-thrust nozzle

Electromagnetic gyros

Deflector shield generator

Reactant injector

Turbo impeller

THE DOG-FIGHTING EDGE

The X-wing achieves its remarkable maneuverability through a combination of three factors. Differential thrust from its four fusial ion engines is the first. High-mass electromagnetic gyros in each of the four retro thrusters add a turning effect that helps to swing the ship in tight curves. Finally, precise bursts of retro-thrust fire forward through the turbine nozzles to add further control and give the ship a critical edge in combat.

Exhaust nozzle

Hyperdrive

Deflector shield projectors

Upper laser cannon mount

Fusial thrust engine

Targeting computer screen (switched off)

Acceleration compensator

Power converters rephase energy for ship subsystems

Cargo bay

Power generator

Power coupling

LASER CANNONS

The X-wing's laser generators operate at the limits of safety to generate maximum destructive power. The long cannons of the X-wing develop longer range for its lasers, which can engage an oncoming enemy before the enemy can return fire.

Laser cannon

Laser cooling sleeve

Laser generator

Magnetic flashback suppressors keep the occasional unstable laserbolt from damaging the cannon

BLT-A4 Y-WING

T HE KOENSAYR Y-WING design dates back many years, as do most of the Y-wings in the Rebel Alliance space combat fleet. The ship is a combination fighter and light bomber, built to last and made to last even longer by dedicated Rebel mechanics. It has earned its reputation as the workhorse of the Rebel fighting forces, and is still the most numerous fighter in the Alliance. There are several different models, adapted for different missions, including one-man and two-man versions. Sporting heavy laser cannons, ion cannons, and proton torpedo magazines, the ship carries devastating firepower, and its solid construction weathers combat damage that would destroy lighter craft. It is neither the fastest nor the most maneuverable ship in the sky, but with its balance of capabilities the Y-wing remains a sturdy asset to the Alliance space combat forces.

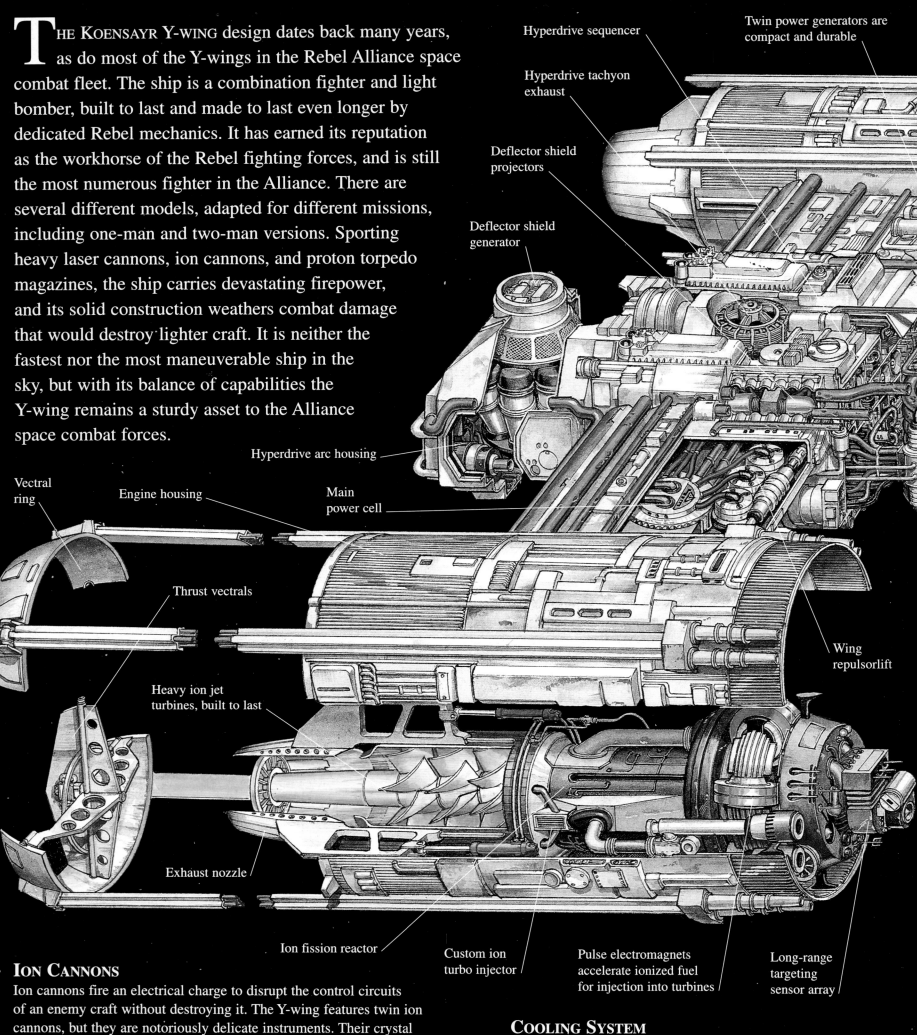

Hyperdrive sequencer

Hyperdrive tachyon exhaust

Deflector shield projectors

Deflector shield generator

Twin power generators are compact and durable

Hyperdrive arc housing

Vectral ring

Engine housing

Main power cell

Thrust vectrals

Heavy ion jet turbines, built to last

Wing repulsorlift

Exhaust nozzle

Ion fission reactor

Custom ion turbo injector

Pulse electromagnets accelerate ionized fuel for injection into turbines

Long-range targeting sensor array

ION CANNONS

Ion cannons fire an electrical charge to disrupt the control circuits of an enemy craft without destroying it. The Y-wing features twin ion cannons, but they are notoriously delicate instruments. Their crystal matrices invariably get vibrated out of alignment in flight and combat, and Rebel mechanics hate them for the time they cost in maintenance. For the attack koen the Death Star, only two Y-wings in the entire Rebel force had functioning ion cannons. These proved critically useful, and one of these craft was the only Y-wing to survive the battle.

COOLING SYSTEM

The Y-wing runs very hot for a ship of its size, and employs a complicated cooling system which runs throughout the ship. Parts of this system need maintenance after every flight. Coolant tubes are often jerry-rigged by Rebel mechanics when leaks render inaccessible sections frustratingly inoperative.

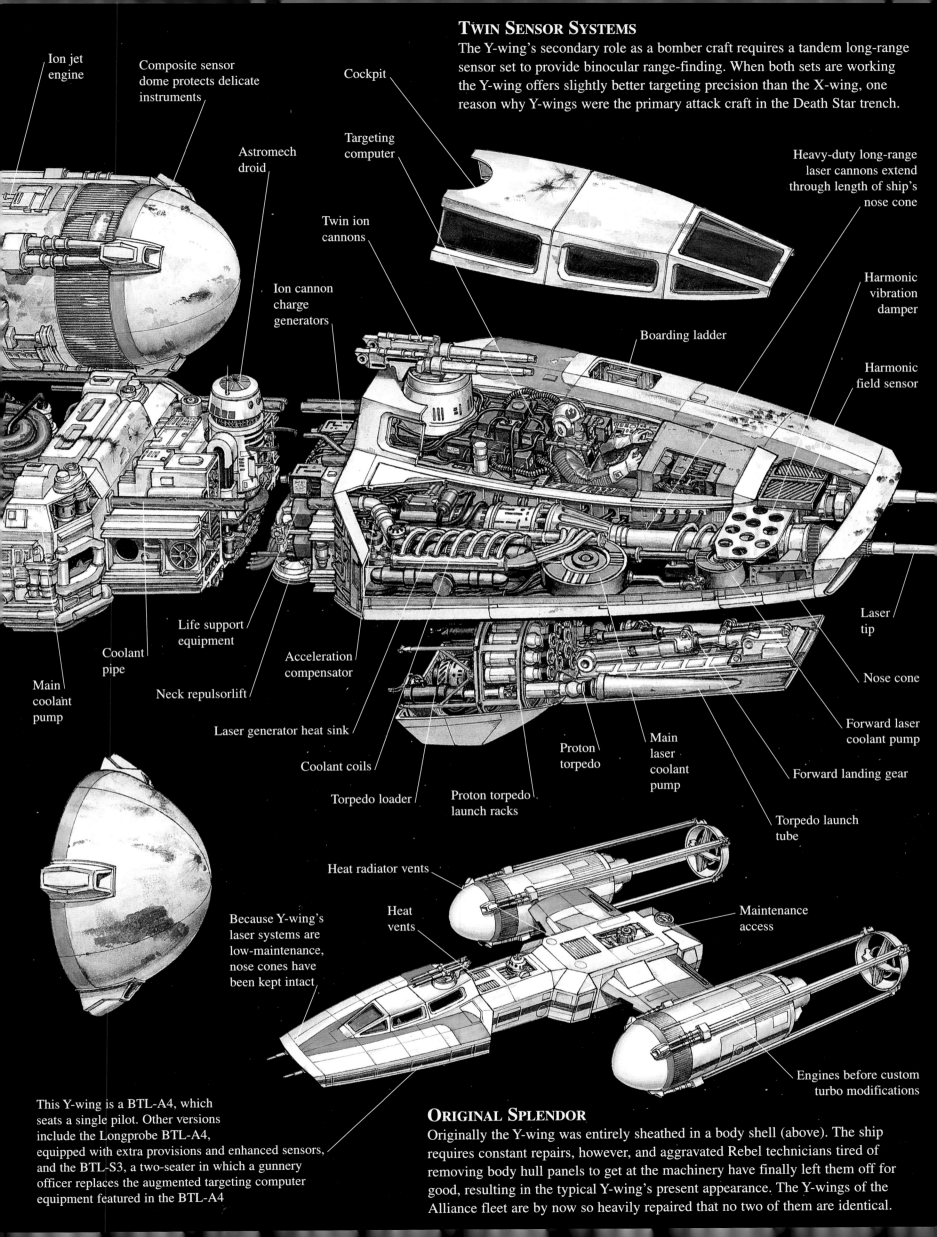

Ion jet engine

Composite sensor dome protects delicate instruments

Astromech droid

Cockpit

Targeting computer

Twin ion cannons

Ion cannon charge generators

TWIN SENSOR SYSTEMS

The Y-wing's secondary role as a bomber craft requires a tandem long-range sensor set to provide binocular range-finding. When both sets are working the Y-wing offers slightly better targeting precision than the X-wing, one reason why Y-wings were the primary attack craft in the Death Star trench.

Heavy-duty long-range laser cannons extend through length of ship's nose cone

Boarding ladder

Harmonic vibration damper

Harmonic field sensor

Main coolant pump

Coolant pipe

Life support equipment

Neck repulsorlift

Acceleration compensator

Laser generator heat sink

Coolant coils

Torpedo loader

Proton torpedo launch racks

Proton torpedo

Main laser coolant pump

Torpedo launch tube

Laser tip

Nose cone

Forward laser coolant pump

Forward landing gear

Heat radiator vents

Heat vents

Because Y-wing's laser systems are low-maintenance, nose cones have been kept intact

Maintenance access

Engines before custom turbo modifications

This Y-wing is a BTL-A4, which seats a single pilot. Other versions include the Longprobe BTL-A4, equipped with extra provisions and enhanced sensors, and the BTL-S3, a two-seater in which a gunnery officer replaces the augmented targeting computer equipment featured in the BTL-A4

ORIGINAL SPLENDOR

Originally the Y-wing was entirely sheathed in a body shell (above). The ship requires constant repairs, however, and aggravated Rebel technicians tired of removing body hull panels to get at the machinery have finally left them off for good, resulting in the typical Y-wing's present appearance. The Y-wings of the Alliance fleet are by now so heavily repaired that no two of them are identical.

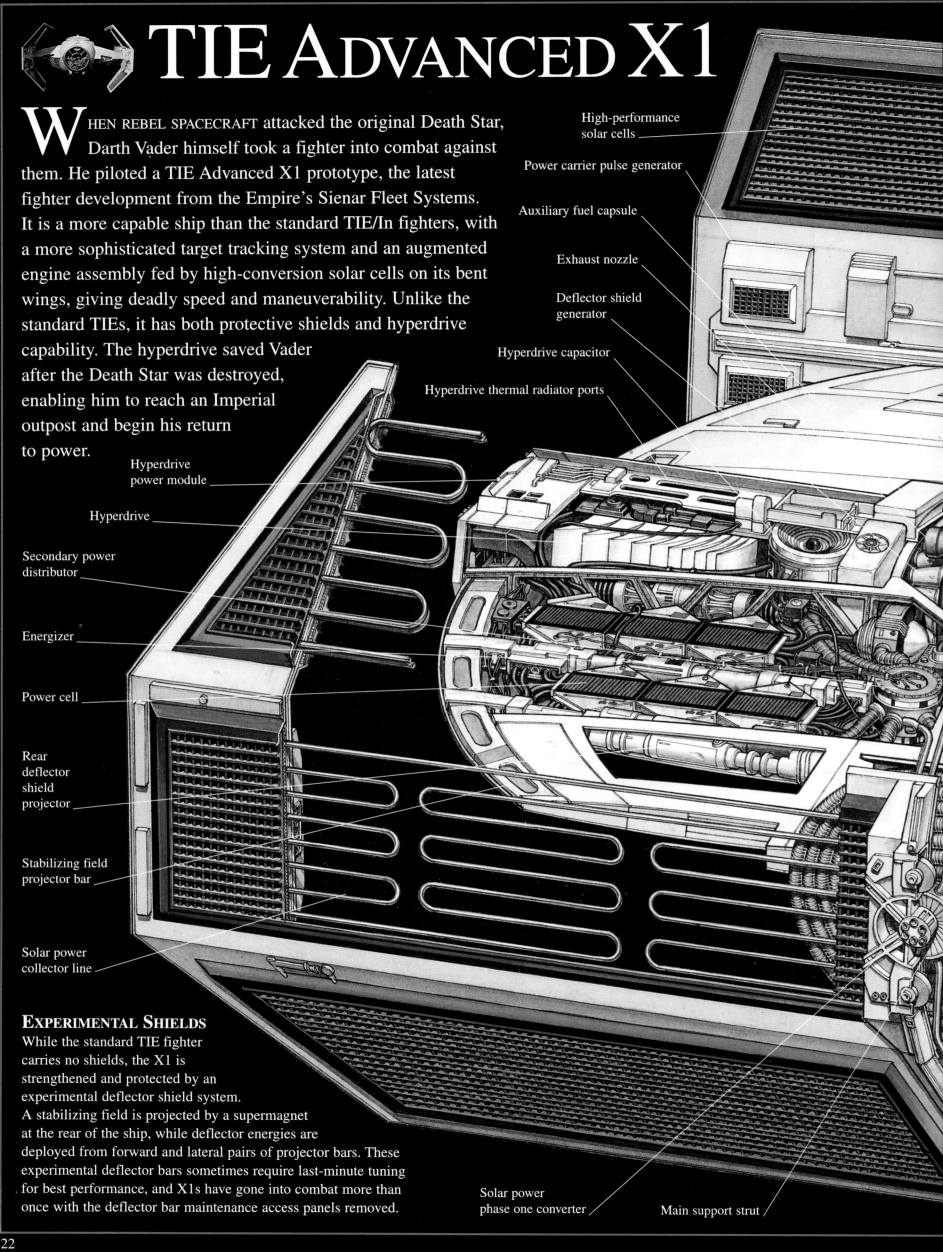

TIE ADVANCED X1

WHEN REBEL SPACECRAFT attacked the original Death Star, Darth Vader himself took a fighter into combat against them. He piloted a TIE Advanced X1 prototype, the latest fighter development from the Empire's Sienar Fleet Systems. It is a more capable ship than the standard TIE/In fighters, with a more sophisticated target tracking system and an augmented engine assembly fed by high-conversion solar cells on its bent wings, giving deadly speed and maneuverability. Unlike the standard TIEs, it has both protective shields and hyperdrive capability. The hyperdrive saved Vader after the Death Star was destroyed, enabling him to reach an Imperial outpost and begin his return to power.

High-performance solar cells

Power carrier pulse generator

Auxiliary fuel capsule

Exhaust nozzle

Deflector shield generator

Hyperdrive capacitor

Hyperdrive thermal radiator ports

Hyperdrive power module

Hyperdrive

Secondary power distributor

Energizer

Power cell

Rear deflector shield projector

Stabilizing field projector bar

Solar power collector line

EXPERIMENTAL SHIELDS

While the standard TIE fighter carries no shields, the X1 is strengthened and protected by an experimental deflector shield system. A stabilizing field is projected by a supermagnet at the rear of the ship, while deflector energies are deployed from forward and lateral pairs of projector bars. These experimental deflector bars sometimes require last-minute tuning for best performance, and X1s have gone into combat more than once with the deflector bar maintenance access panels removed.

Solar power phase one converter

Main support strut

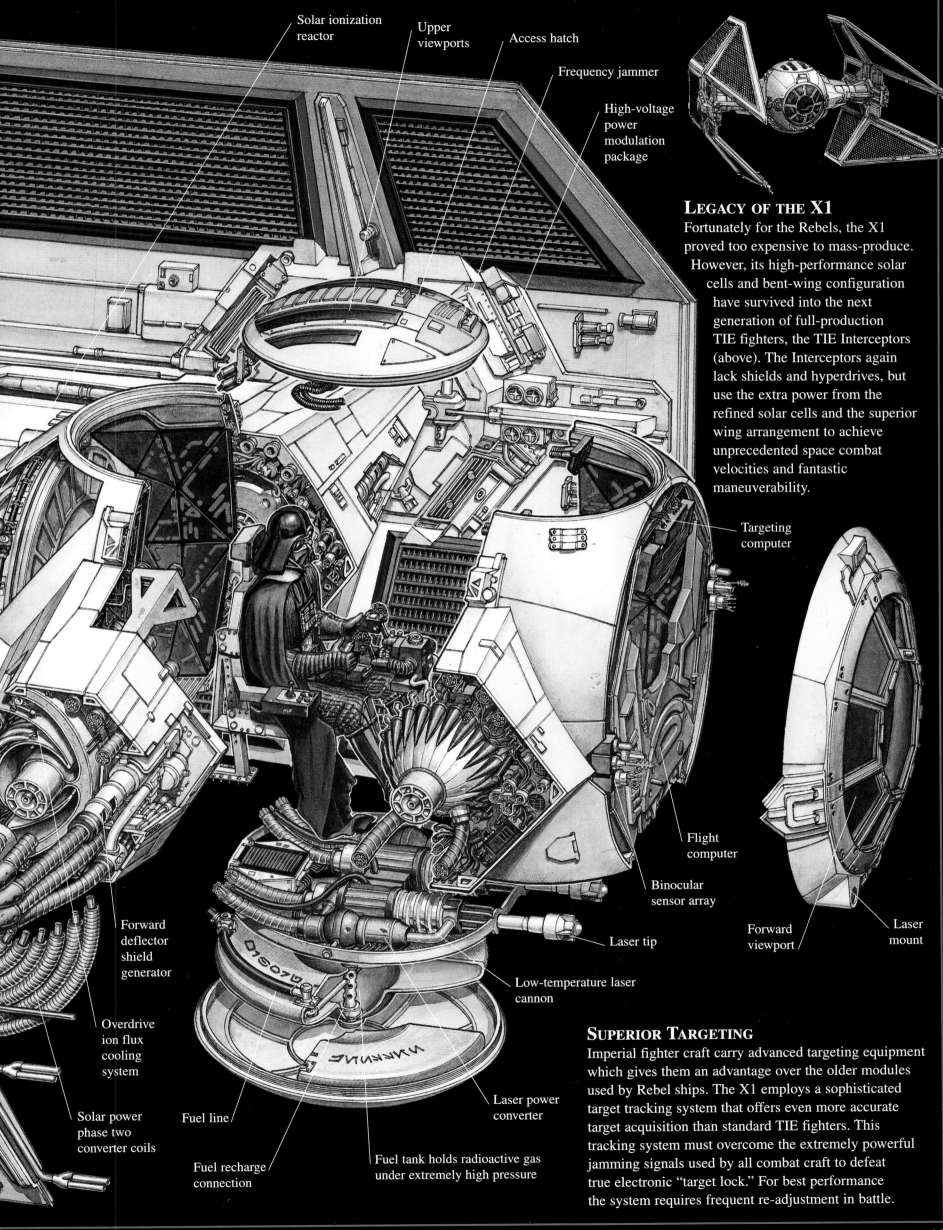

Solar ionization reactor

Upper viewports

Access hatch

Frequency jammer

High-voltage power modulation package

LEGACY OF THE X1

Fortunately for the Rebels, the X1 proved too expensive to mass-produce. However, its high-performance solar cells and bent-wing configuration have survived into the next generation of full-production TIE fighters, the TIE Interceptors (above). The Interceptors again lack shields and hyperdrives, but use the extra power from the refined solar cells and the superior wing arrangement to achieve unprecedented space combat velocities and fantastic maneuverability.

Targeting computer

Flight computer

Binocular sensor array

Forward deflector shield generator

Forward viewport

Laser mount

Laser tip

Overdrive ion flux cooling system

Low-temperature laser cannon

Solar power phase two converter coils

Fuel line

Laser power converter

SUPERIOR TARGETING

Imperial fighter craft carry advanced targeting equipment which gives them an advantage over the older modules used by Rebel ships. The X1 employs a sophisticated target tracking system that offers even more accurate target acquisition than standard TIE fighters. This tracking system must overcome the extremely powerful jamming signals used by all combat craft to defeat true electronic "target lock." For best performance the system requires frequent re-adjustment in battle.

Fuel recharge connection

Fuel tank holds radioactive gas under extremely high pressure

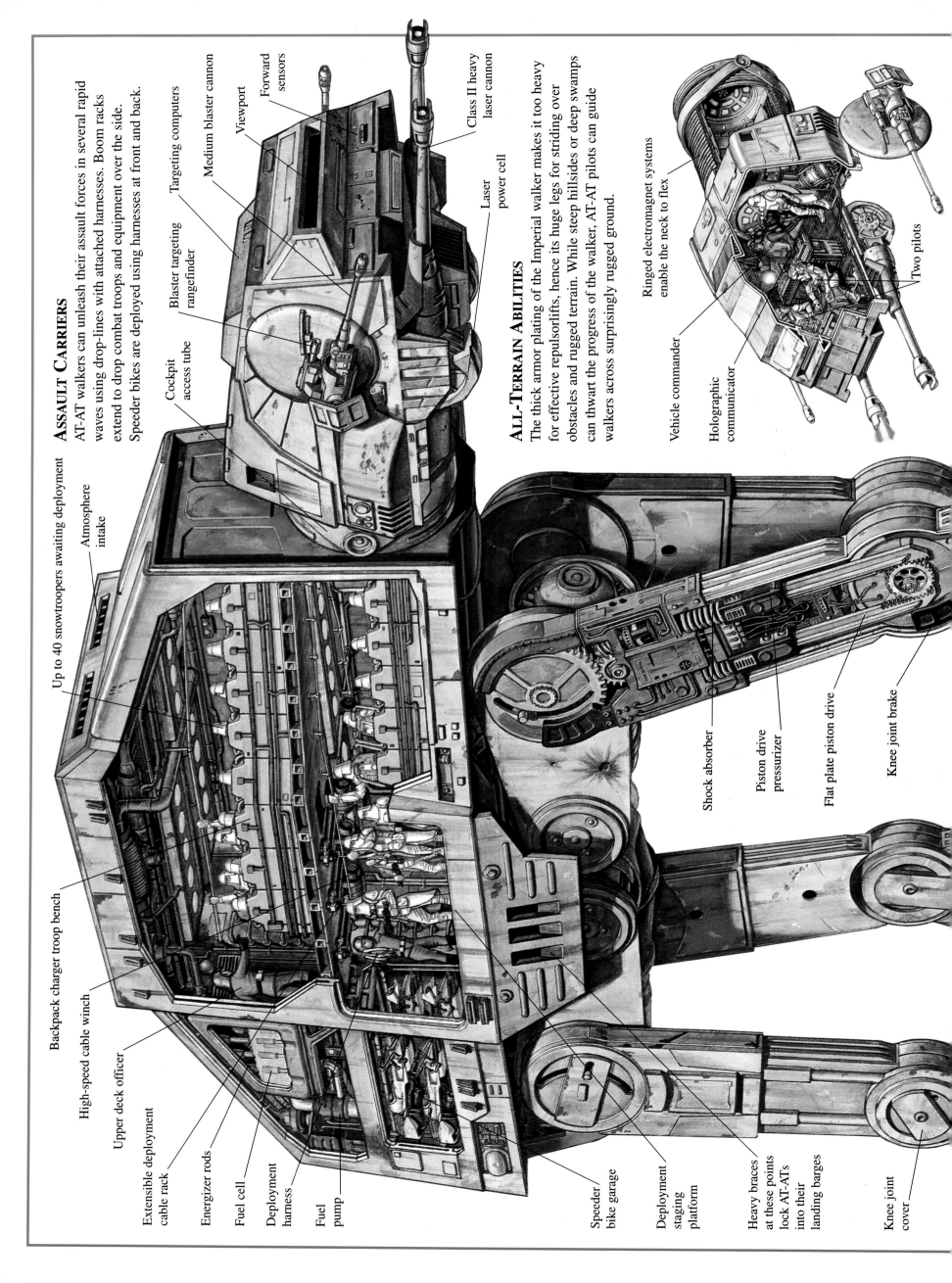

ASSAULT CARRIERS

AT-AT walkers can unleash their assault forces in several rapid waves using drop-lines with attached harnesses. Boom racks extend to drop combat troops and equipment over the side. Speeder bikes are deployed using harnesses at front and back.

Forward sensors

Class II heavy laser cannon

Medium blaster cannon

Viewport

Targeting computers

Blaster targeting rangefinder

Cockpit access tube

Laser power cell

Up to 40 snowtroopers awaiting deployment

Atmosphere intake

Backpack charger troop bench

High-speed cable winch

Upper deck officer

Extensible deployment cable rack

Energizer rods

Fuel cell

Deployment harness

Fuel pump

Speeder bike garage

Deployment staging platform

Heavy braces at these points lock AT-ATs into their landing barges

Knee joint cover

ALL-TERRAIN ABILITIES

The thick armor plating of the Imperial walker makes it too heavy for effective repulsorlifts, hence its huge legs for striding over obstacles and rugged terrain. While steep hillsides or deep swamps can thwart the progress of the walker, AT-AT pilots can guide walkers across surprisingly rugged ground.

Ringed electromagnet systems enable the neck to flex

Two pilots

Vehicle commander

Holographic communicator

Shock absorber

Piston drive pressurizer

Flat plate piston drive

Knee joint brake

COMMAND COCKPIT

The walker's heavily armored head serves as a cockpit for the two pilots and the vehicle commander. On its exterior are mounted the vehicle's weapons systems. While both pilots are fully qualified to perform all control functions, in normal practice one serves as driver while the other acts as gunner. Firing controls can at any time be yielded to the vehicle commander, who uses a periscope display capable of tactical and photographic readouts. The two pilots are guided by terrain sensors under the cockpit and ground sensors built into the feet of the vehicle. Scans read the nature and shape of the terrain ahead, assuring infallible footing.

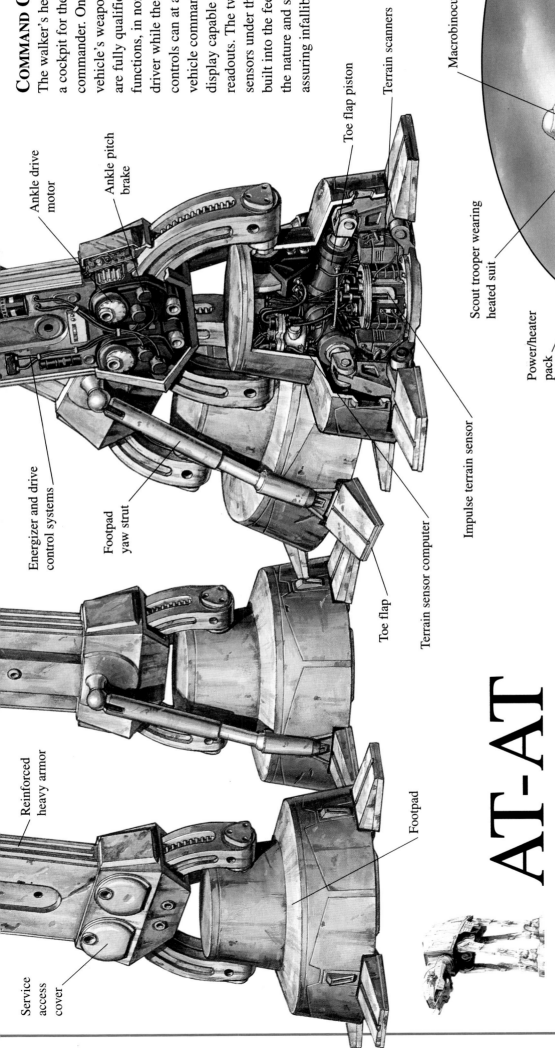

Ankle drive motor

Ankle pitch brake

Toe flap piston

Terrain scanners

Energizer and drive control systems

Footpad yaw strut

Impulse terrain sensor

Toe flap

Terrain sensor computer

Reinforced heavy armor

Footpad

Service access cover

Antipersonnel pursuit gun

Macrobinocular viewplate

Scout trooper wearing heated suit

Power/heater pack

SPEEDER BIKES

AT-AT walkers usually carry a set of high-velocity repulsorlift speeder bikes for scouting or survivor-hunting missions. The speed and agility of these bikes complement the plodding might of the walkers, making the combined assault capability thorough and overwhelming. The colossal size and nightmarish animal resemblance of the AT-AT combine with its combat strengths to give it tremendous psychological power. Until the Battle of Hoth, no army had ever fought resolutely against an onslaught of walkers, so frightening and devastating is their presence.

AT-AT

Deployed as weapons of terror, the gigantic Imperial All Terrain Armored Transport walkers advance inexorably on the battlefield like unstoppable giants. These behemoth monsters are shielded with heavy armor cladding, making them invulnerable to all but the heaviest turbolaser weaponry. Blaster bolts from ordinary turrets and cannons merely glance off the walker's armor or are harmlessly absorbed and dissipated. A powerful reactor produces the raw energy needed to move this weighty battle machine. Cannons in the movable cockpit spit death and savagery at helpless foes below, cutting a swath of destruction which the mighty footpads then crash through. Breaking enemy lines with its blaster fire and lumbering mass, the walker functions as a troop carrier, holding in its body platoons of crack assault soldiers, ground weaponry, and speeder bike antipersonnel/reconnaissance vehicles. When this cargo of terror is released into the chaos and destruction a walker has created, another Imperial victory is nearly complete.

SNOWSPEEDER

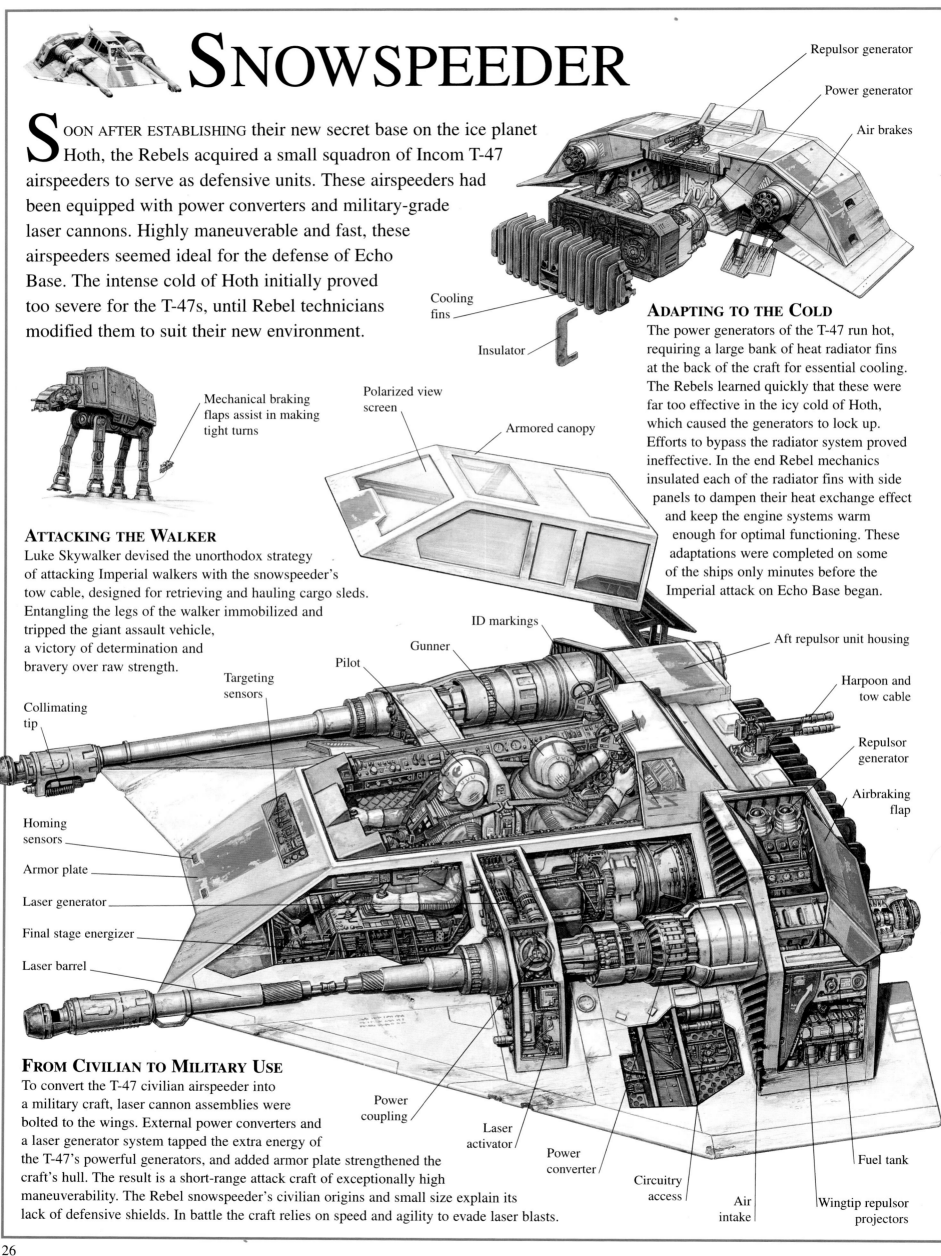

SOON AFTER ESTABLISHING their new secret base on the ice planet Hoth, the Rebels acquired a small squadron of Incom T-47 airspeeders to serve as defensive units. These airspeeders had been equipped with power converters and military-grade laser cannons. Highly maneuverable and fast, these airspeeders seemed ideal for the defense of Echo Base. The intense cold of Hoth initially proved too severe for the T-47s, until Rebel technicians modified them to suit their new environment.

Repulsor generator

Power generator

Air brakes

Cooling fins

Insulator

ADAPTING TO THE COLD

The power generators of the T-47 run hot, requiring a large bank of heat radiator fins at the back of the craft for essential cooling. The Rebels learned quickly that these were far too effective in the icy cold of Hoth, which caused the generators to lock up. Efforts to bypass the radiator system proved ineffective. In the end Rebel mechanics insulated each of the radiator fins with side panels to dampen their heat exchange effect and keep the engine systems warm enough for optimal functioning. These adaptations were completed on some of the ships only minutes before the Imperial attack on Echo Base began.

Mechanical braking flaps assist in making tight turns

Polarized view screen

Armored canopy

ATTACKING THE WALKER

Luke Skywalker devised the unorthodox strategy of attacking Imperial walkers with the snowspeeder's tow cable, designed for retrieving and hauling cargo sleds. Entangling the legs of the walker immobilized and tripped the giant assault vehicle, a victory of determination and bravery over raw strength.

ID markings

Gunner

Pilot

Aft repulsor unit housing

Targeting sensors

Harpoon and tow cable

Collimating tip

Repulsor generator

Homing sensors

Airbraking flap

Armor plate

Laser generator

Final stage energizer

Laser barrel

FROM CIVILIAN TO MILITARY USE

To convert the T-47 civilian airspeeder into a military craft, laser cannon assemblies were bolted to the wings. External power converters and a laser generator system tapped the extra energy of the T-47's powerful generators, and added armor plate strengthened the craft's hull. The result is a short-range attack craft of exceptionally high maneuverability. The Rebel snowspeeder's civilian origins and small size explain its lack of defensive shields. In battle the craft relies on speed and agility to evade laser blasts.

Power coupling

Laser activator

Power converter

Circuitry access

Air intake

Fuel tank

Wingtip repulsor projectors

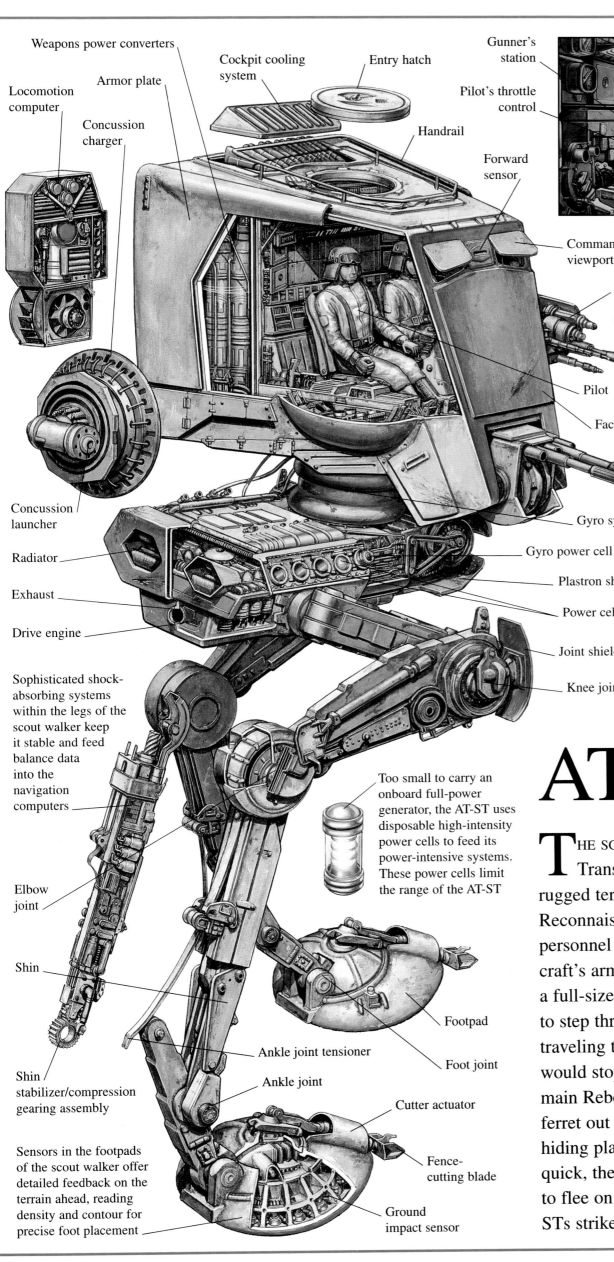

Weapons power converters

Locomotion computer

Armor plate

Concussion charger

Cockpit cooling system

Entry hatch

Gunner's station

Pilot's throttle control

Handrail

Forward sensor

Command viewport

THE COCKPIT VIEW

Viewscreens and holo-projectors allow AT-ST crew to see ahead and behind simultaneously. While the computer can guide the scout walker over even ground, an expert human pilot must balance the wide variety of data input and control the craft's walking in difficult terrain.

Light blaster cannon

Pilot

Face armor

Twin blaster cannons

GYRO STABILIZED

With an expert pilot at the helm, an AT-ST can move with remarkable agility across a wide variety of terrain. A powerful gyro stabilizer coupled with a complex locomotion system allows the scout walker to mimic the walking movements of a living creature.

Concussion launcher

Radiator

Exhaust

Drive engine

Gyro system

Gyro power cell

Plastron shield

Power cells

Joint shield

Knee joint

Sophisticated shock-absorbing systems within the legs of the scout walker keep it stable and feed balance data into the navigation computers

Too small to carry an onboard full-power generator, the AT-ST uses disposable high-intensity power cells to feed its power-intensive systems. These power cells limit the range of the AT-ST

Elbow joint

Shin

Shin stabilizer/compression gearing assembly

Footpad

Foot joint

Sensors in the footpads of the scout walker offer detailed feedback on the terrain ahead, reading density and contour for precise foot placement

Ankle joint tensioner

Ankle joint

Cutter actuator

Fence-cutting blade

Ground impact sensor

AT-ST

T HE SCOUT WALKER, or All Terrain Scout Transport (AT-ST) walks easily through rugged terrain to carry out its missions. Reconnaissance, battle line support, and anti-personnel hunting make excellent use of the craft's armaments and capabilities. Faster than a full-size AT-AT, the scout walker is also able to step through denser terrain with greater ease, traveling through small canyons or forest that would stop an AT-AT. While AT-ATs crush main Rebel defensive emplacements, AT-STs ferret out small pockets of resistance or the hiding places of enemy soldiers. Agile and quick, the scout walker is almost impossible to flee on foot, and the sight of patrolling AT-STs strikes fear into isolated ground troops.

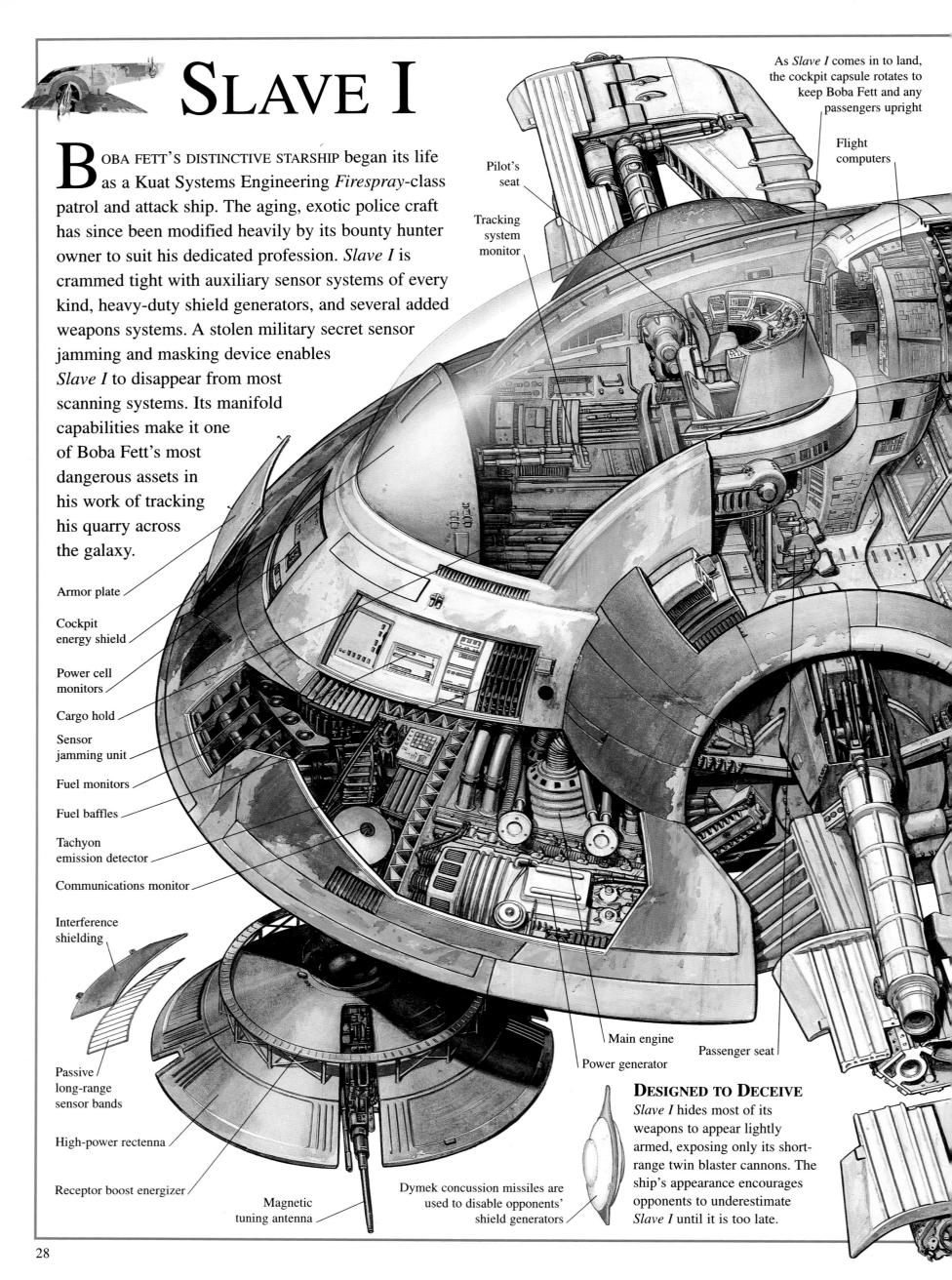

SLAVE I

BOBA FETT'S DISTINCTIVE STARSHIP began its life as a Kuat Systems Engineering *Firespray*-class patrol and attack ship. The aging, exotic police craft has since been modified heavily by its bounty hunter owner to suit his dedicated profession. *Slave I* is crammed tight with auxiliary sensor systems of every kind, heavy-duty shield generators, and several added weapons systems. A stolen military secret sensor jamming and masking device enables *Slave I* to disappear from most scanning systems. Its manifold capabilities make it one of Boba Fett's most dangerous assets in his work of tracking his quarry across the galaxy.

Armor plate

Cockpit energy shield

Power cell monitors

Cargo hold

Sensor jamming unit

Fuel monitors

Fuel baffles

Tachyon emission detector

Communications monitor

Interference shielding

Passive long-range sensor bands

High-power rectenna

Receptor boost energizer

Magnetic tuning antenna

Pilot's seat

Tracking system monitor

As *Slave I* comes in to land, the cockpit capsule rotates to keep Boba Fett and any passengers upright

Flight computers

Main engine

Power generator

Passenger seat

Dymek concussion missiles are used to disable opponents' shield generators

DESIGNED TO DECEIVE

Slave I hides most of its weapons to appear lightly armed, exposing only its short-range twin blaster cannons. The ship's appearance encourages opponents to underestimate *Slave I* until it is too late.

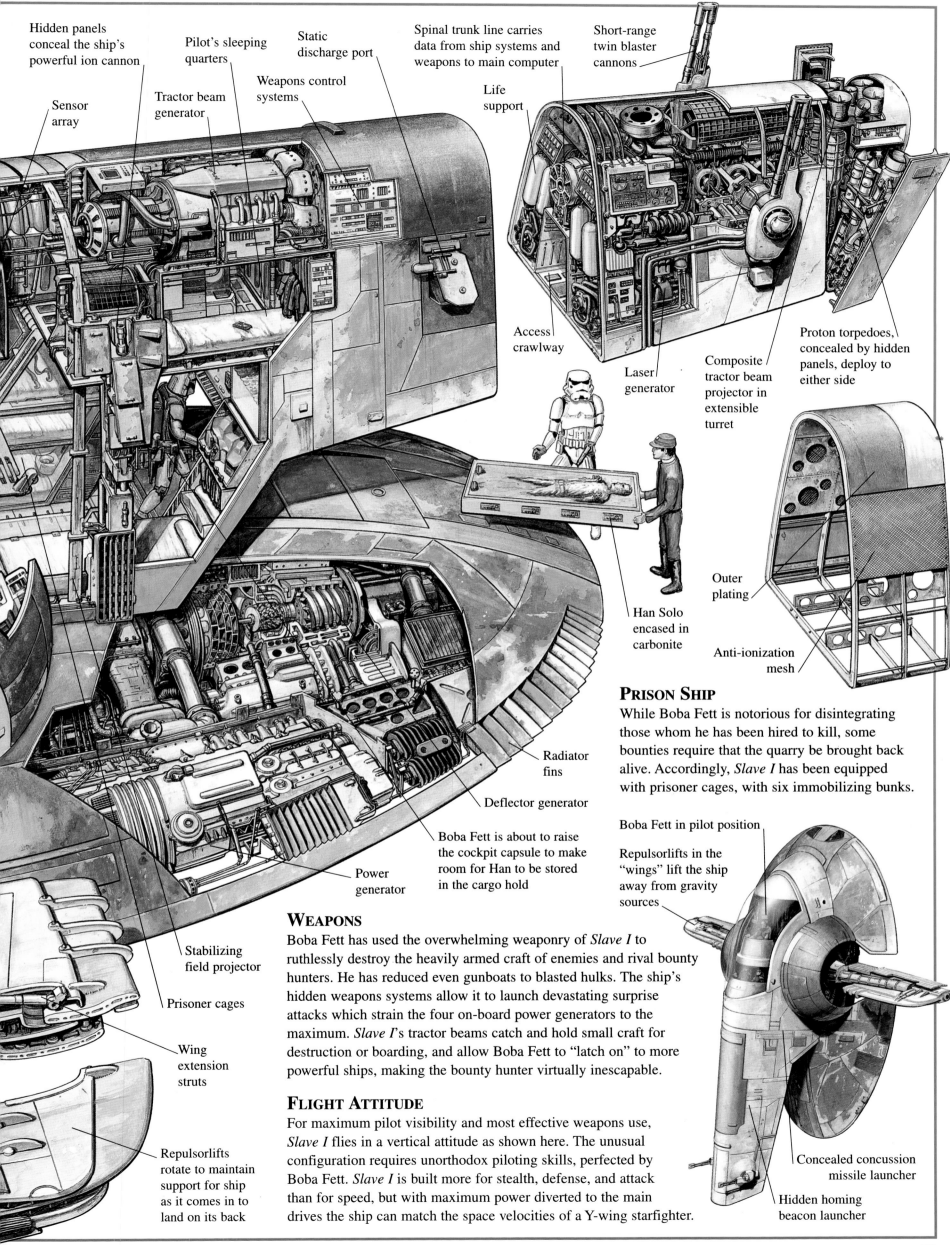

Hidden panels conceal the ship's powerful ion cannon

Pilot's sleeping quarters

Static discharge port

Weapons control systems

Spinal trunk line carries data from ship systems and weapons to main computer

Short-range twin blaster cannons

Sensor array

Tractor beam generator

Life support

Access crawlway

Laser generator

Composite tractor beam projector in extensible turret

Proton torpedoes, concealed by hidden panels, deploy to either side

Outer plating

Anti-ionization mesh

Han Solo encased in carbonite

Radiator fins

Deflector generator

Boba Fett is about to raise the cockpit capsule to make room for Han to be stored in the cargo hold

Power generator

Stabilizing field projector

Prisoner cages

Wing extension struts

Repulsorlifts rotate to maintain support for ship as it comes in to land on its back

PRISON SHIP

While Boba Fett is notorious for disintegrating those whom he has been hired to kill, some bounties require that the quarry be brought back alive. Accordingly, *Slave I* has been equipped with prisoner cages, with six immobilizing bunks.

Boba Fett in pilot position

Repulsorlifts in the "wings" lift the ship away from gravity sources

WEAPONS

Boba Fett has used the overwhelming weaponry of *Slave I* to ruthlessly destroy the heavily armed craft of enemies and rival bounty hunters. He has reduced even gunboats to blasted hulks. The ship's hidden weapons systems allow it to launch devastating surprise attacks which strain the four on-board power generators to the maximum. *Slave I*'s tractor beams catch and hold small craft for destruction or boarding, and allow Boba Fett to "latch on" to more powerful ships, making the bounty hunter virtually inescapable.

FLIGHT ATTITUDE

For maximum pilot visibility and most effective weapons use, *Slave I* flies in a vertical attitude as shown here. The unusual configuration requires unorthodox piloting skills, perfected by Boba Fett. *Slave I* is built more for stealth, defense, and attack than for speed, but with maximum power diverted to the main drives the ship can match the space velocities of a Y-wing starfighter.

Concealed concussion missile launcher

Hidden homing beacon launcher

JABBA'S SAIL BARGE

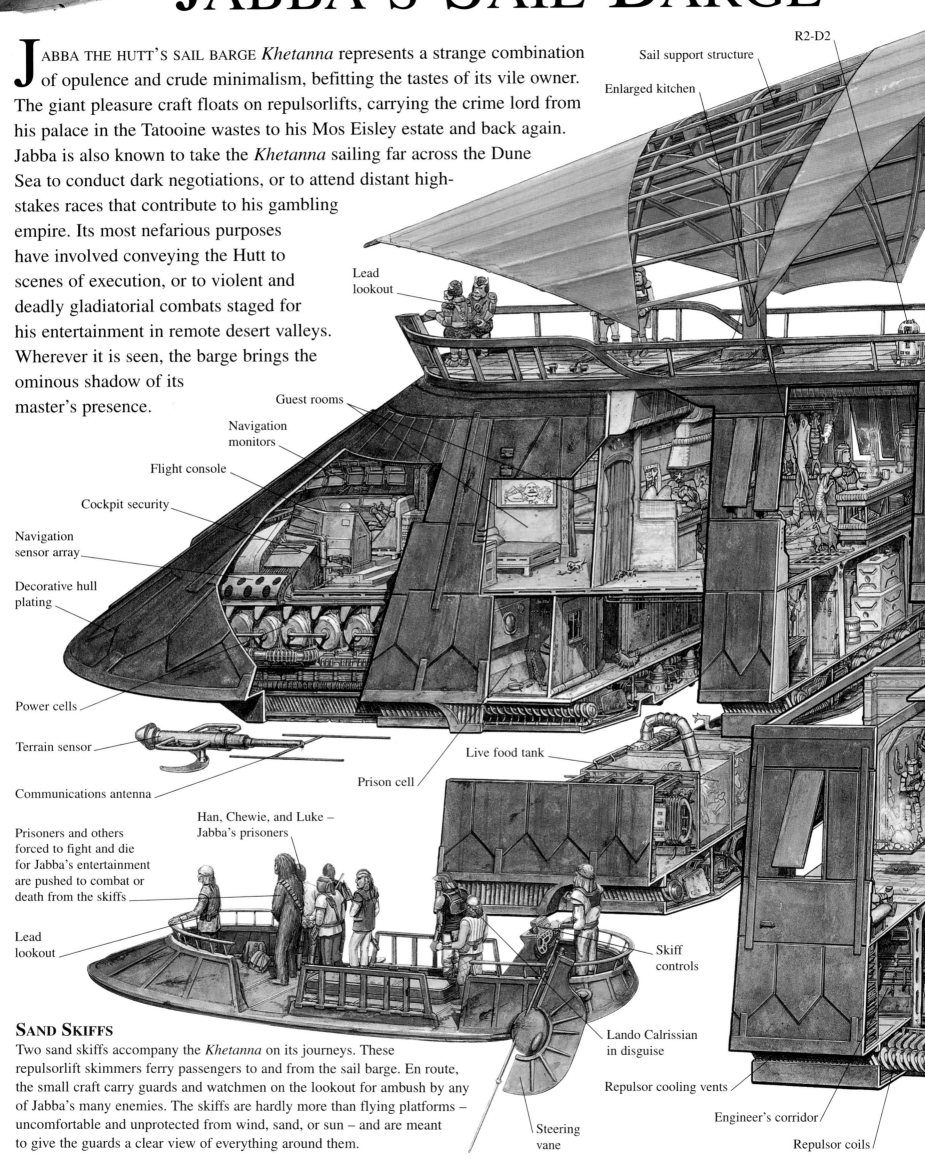

JABBA THE HUTT'S SAIL BARGE *Khetanna* represents a strange combination of opulence and crude minimalism, befitting the tastes of its vile owner. The giant pleasure craft floats on repulsorlifts, carrying the crime lord from his palace in the Tatooine wastes to his Mos Eisley estate and back again. Jabba is also known to take the *Khetanna* sailing far across the Dune Sea to conduct dark negotiations, or to attend distant high-stakes races that contribute to his gambling empire. Its most nefarious purposes have involved conveying the Hutt to scenes of execution, or to violent and deadly gladiatorial combats staged for his entertainment in remote desert valleys. Wherever it is seen, the barge brings the ominous shadow of its master's presence.

R2-D2

Sail support structure

Enlarged kitchen

Lead lookout

Guest rooms

Navigation monitors

Flight console

Cockpit security

Navigation sensor array

Decorative hull plating

Power cells

Terrain sensor

Communications antenna

Live food tank

Prison cell

Prisoners and others forced to fight and die for Jabba's entertainment are pushed to combat or death from the skiffs

Han, Chewie, and Luke – Jabba's prisoners

Lead lookout

Skiff controls

Lando Calrissian in disguise

SAND SKIFFS

Two sand skiffs accompany the *Khetanna* on its journeys. These repulsorlift skimmers ferry passengers to and from the sail barge. En route, the small craft carry guards and watchmen on the lookout for ambush by any of Jabba's many enemies. The skiffs are hardly more than flying platforms – uncomfortable and unprotected from wind, sand, or sun – and are meant to give the guards a clear view of everything around them.

Repulsor cooling vents

Engineer's corridor

Steering vane

Repulsor coils

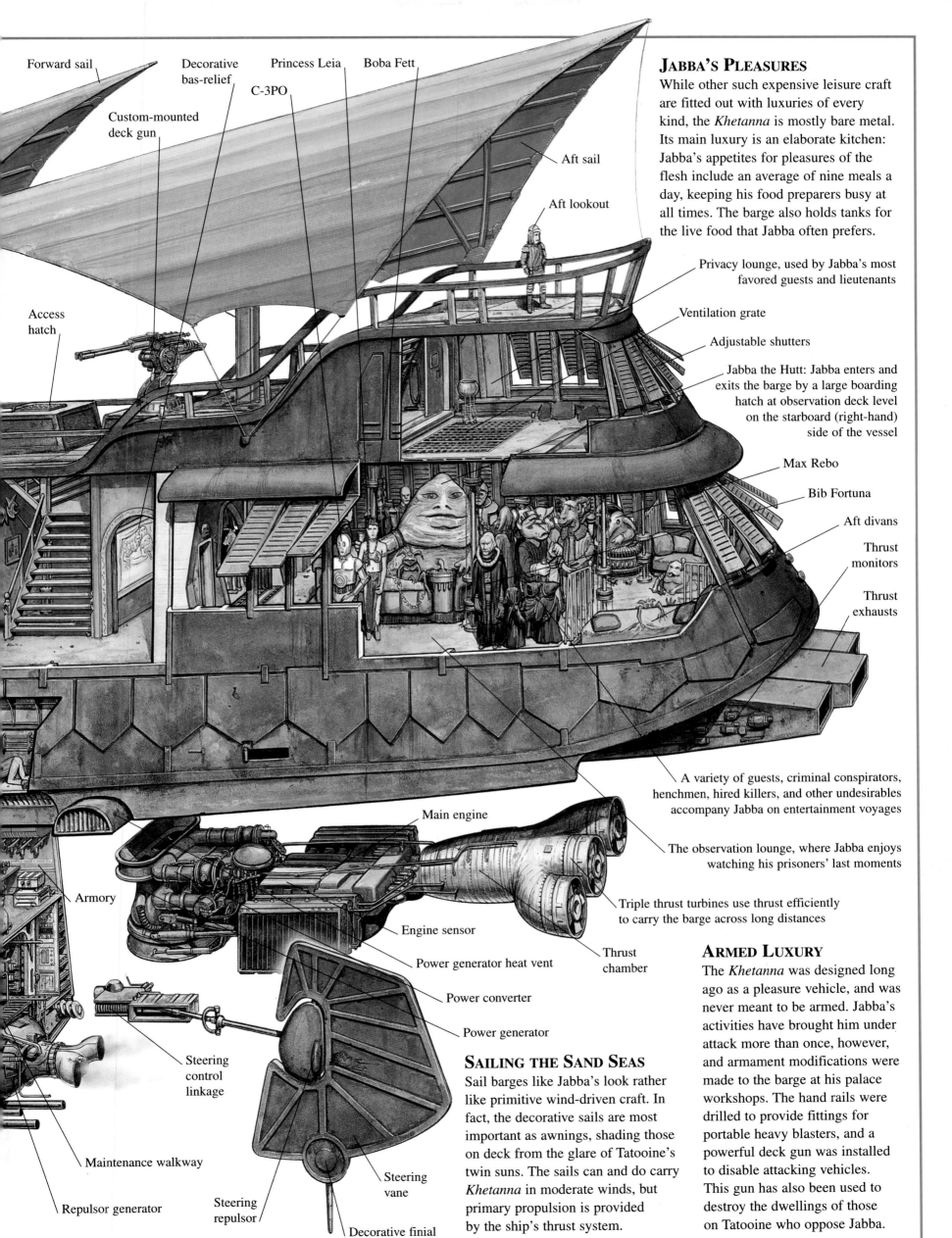

Forward sail

Decorative bas-relief

Princess Leia

Boba Fett

Custom-mounted deck gun

C-3PO

Aft sail

Aft lookout

Access hatch

JABBA'S PLEASURES

While other such expensive leisure craft are fitted out with luxuries of every kind, the *Khetanna* is mostly bare metal. Its main luxury is an elaborate kitchen: Jabba's appetites for pleasures of the flesh include an average of nine meals a day, keeping his food preparers busy at all times. The barge also holds tanks for the live food that Jabba often prefers.

Privacy lounge, used by Jabba's most favored guests and lieutenants

Ventilation grate

Adjustable shutters

Jabba the Hutt: Jabba enters and exits the barge by a large boarding hatch at observation deck level on the starboard (right-hand) side of the vessel

Max Rebo

Bib Fortuna

Aft divans

Thrust monitors

Thrust exhausts

A variety of guests, criminal conspirators, henchmen, hired killers, and other undesirables accompany Jabba on entertainment voyages

The observation lounge, where Jabba enjoys watching his prisoners' last moments

Main engine

Armory

Engine sensor

Power generator heat vent

Power converter

Power generator

Triple thrust turbines use thrust efficiently to carry the barge across long distances

Thrust chamber

ARMED LUXURY

The *Khetanna* was designed long ago as a pleasure vehicle, and was never meant to be armed. Jabba's activities have brought him under attack more than once, however, and armament modifications were made to the barge at his palace workshops. The hand rails were drilled to provide fittings for portable heavy blasters, and a powerful deck gun was installed to disable attacking vehicles. This gun has also been used to destroy the dwellings of those on Tatooine who oppose Jabba.

Steering control linkage

Maintenance walkway

Repulsor generator

Steering repulsor

Steering vane

Decorative finial

SAILING THE SAND SEAS

Sail barges like Jabba's look rather like primitive wind-driven craft. In fact, the decorative sails are most important as awnings, shading those on deck from the glare of Tatooine's twin suns. The sails can and do carry *Khetanna* in moderate winds, but primary propulsion is provided by the ship's thrust system.

A DK PUBLISHING BOOK

PROJECT ART EDITOR Iain Morris
PROJECT EDITOR David Pickering
US EDITOR Jane Mason
MANAGING ART EDITOR Cathy Tincknell
DTP DESIGNER Kim Browne
PRODUCTION Louise Barrett, Katy Holmes, & Steve Lang

First American Edition, 1998
2 4 6 8 10 9 7 5 3 1
Published in the United States by
DK Publishing, Inc.
95 Madison Avenue
New York, New York 10016

Visit us on the World Wide Web at
http://www.starwars.com   http://www.dk.com

Library of Congress Cataloging-in-Publication Data
Reynolds, David West.
Star Wars: Incredible cross-sections / by David West Reynolds. — 1st American ed.
p.   cm.
Includes index.
ISBN 0-7894-3480-6
1. Star Wars films—Pictorial works—Juvenile literature.
I. Title
PN1995.9.S695R48   1998
791.43'75—dc21   98-22878
                                               CIP

Color reproduction by Colourscan, Singapore
Printed in Italy by A. Mondadori Editore, Verona

Acknowledgements
Hans Jenssen painted the X-wing, Y-wing, *Millennium Falcon*, TIE Advanced X1, Death Star, TIE fighter, Blockade Runner, and AT-AT.
Richard Chasemore painted Jabba's Sail Barge, *Slave I*, Snowspeeder, AT-ST, Star Destroyer, and Sandcrawler.
Dorling Kindersley would like to thank Nick Turpin, Will Lach, and Connie Robinson for editorial assistance and Anne Sharples for design assistance.
The author would like to extend special thanks to the artists, who were first-rate collaborators on this project, and also to
Curtis J. Saxton and Robert B. K. Brown for their excellent technical commentaries on *Star Wars* spacecraft.

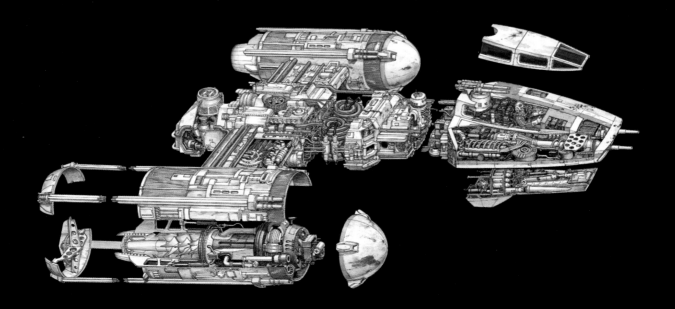